For All My Readers

Also by Cynthia Wall

NIGHT SIGNALS

HOSTAGE IN THE WOODS

FIREWATCH!

EASY TARGET

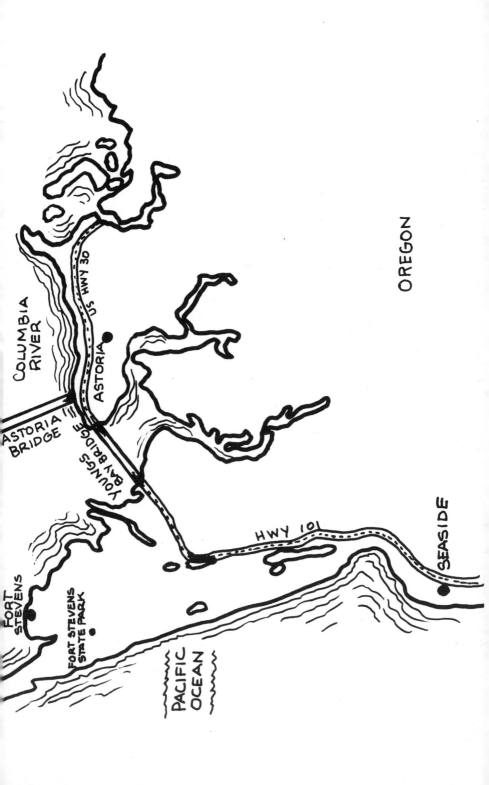

Chapter 1

Magic Schemes

Friday, June 26th 3 p.m.
Ensenada

Orlando smiled with satisfaction at his reflection in the mirror. He added a final dab of cosmetic glue to a protruding edge of his fake black mustache and ran a comb through his shock of dark glistening hair.

"What do you think, Ferdy? Am I Orlando the Great?"

The younger man glanced up at him, a mixture of fear and disbelief on his face. He shook his head and continued struggling into the crisp formal white attire of a shipboard dining room waiter while Orlando practiced arching his eyebrows and grimacing at himself in the mirror.

Finally done with his black bow tie, Ferdy glanced up at him and laughed nervously.

"I can't believe you're actually doing this. How'd you fool them at the cruise line?" "Nothing to fool. Remember, Orlando had those great recommendations. People in the cruise office seemed impressed. I am Orlando. Even been living in his apartment for the past six months. I don't think his neighbors even knew him. Only one asked me who I was and I told her I was his brother. Said that Orlando had gone to Sicily to be with our sick mother — that I would be going there eventually too

"There's more to being a magician than recommendations. Let's see you do a trick. How 'bout that, huh?"

To Ferdy's surprise, Orlando produced a deck of cards from his pocket. He spread them on the table and asked Ferdy to pick one. He even had him sign his name on it.

Then he solemnly placed the card in an envelope, put it on an ashtray, and lit the edge of the envelope with his cigarette lighter. The waiter watched silently, a smirk of disbelief on his face. But that expression turned to amazement as Orlando reached up his sleeve and produced Ferdy's signed card.

"Hey, how you'd do that?"

"Magic," Orlando replied with an evil grin. "I had a cellmate who taught me all sorts of tricks. Now tell me what you've learned about the passengers."

"Here's a ship's list" Ferdy said, producing the long white pages from his narrow closet. "You can pretty much tell from the cabin assignments which parties include children."

The men pored over the list of names. Orlando, pencil in hand, put stars by several of them.

"Who are they?"

"I've been following the L.A. business news for a couple of months ever since I got out of the joint," Orlando replied. "These names look familiar. Like this Grant Gressner guy — party of six. I think he's head of some corporation. Big computer firm if I remember. Or this one — Marlin Sconesby. I know he's big money but just a party of two. Gotta have kids if this trick's gonna work."

"This whole thing scares me."

"As much as going to prison for murder?"

Ferdy's face blanched white and Leo a.k.a. "Orlando" stepped up close to him.

"You listen to me and you listen good. You're going to help me with this gig and then you're a free man. I'm going to disappear and your secret's going with me. I'll be happy and you can go on being a smiling waiter on this tugboat forever if you want."

Ferdy took a deep breath and squared his shoulders. He watched as the new magician studied the list and then hid it in his laundry sack. He finished dressing and told

Orlando he had to report to the dining room. A smile crept over Orlando's face as Ferdy exited the room.

It had been just six months since their fateful meeting on a rainy January night. What for him, Leo Kinelli — now Orlando — had started out as a bring, lonely evening in a bar. Until Ferdy and the real Orlando had entered the scene that is. Intrigued by his own physical resemblance to the man who called himself Orlando, Leo had listened with interest to their conversation.

"So whadya doing here? Ferdy? That what your name is?"

"Yeah. Just visiting my family during the off season."

"Family, huh? Used to have family, but not any more."

The tall man downed the rest of his drink and tapped on the counter for another.

"The only family I had was on the ship, but they're gone too. Said they don't need a magician this season. Not even Orlando the Great. But I got another job, maybe. 'Cuz'I got great recommendations."

He burped loudly and pulled a thick bundle of white papers from his jacket.

"See these, Ferdy. This is my application for Magical Seas — got an interview tomorrow."

"Really?"

Leo's eyes narrowed as he remembered the poker game the two struck up, the argument when Orlando couldn't pay up, and then the fist fight in the alley. He could almost laugh now as he recalled Ferdy's horror-struck expression when he realized that his wildly thrown punch had killed the magician.

That was when he, Leo Kinelli, had stepped up to "help" Ferdy — helped him shove the dead man in a car trunk, helped him bury him on a remote mountain road, and helped him regain his calm. In return for his "help,"

Leo had taken Orlando's documents and pledged his silence to Ferdy.

The new "Orlando" wandered down the narrow crew hall to his small cabin. As a booked performer, he rated a cabin all to himself. Granted it wasn't much, but as he looked around the compact quarters, he laughed. If all went well, he would soon be a multi-millionaire with a villa of his own somewhere in sunny South America. The magic tricks that he had perfected in prison were going to pay off.

The inaugural cruise of the Sea Mystic, a nine day jaunt from Ensenada to Seattle and back. They would be docking in San Francisco for a day and twenty-four hours in Astoria, Oregon to take part in the city's summer music and magic festival. Everything seemed to be falling in place like clockwork — magic clockwork.

He gave a quick peek inside the black duffel bag that held not only his magic tricks but also his phony passport. This time next week... he thought and then cracked his knuckles as he looked out the tiny porthole at the stream of passengers now ascending the gangway.

The Sea Mystic, a 70,000 ton vessel, freshly painted and scrubbed, was almost ready. Tons of food, everything from pizza to papayas, were being loaded through cargo bays. In the ship's belly, four huge diesel engines sat ready to drive the ship through the water at 20 knots. The six p.m. departure was fast approaching.

Orlando watched a steward carrying a tray of bon voyage confetti to the upper deck. The steward nodded to Orlando and Orlando nodded back, but his eyes were focused on the line of passengers approaching the gangplank. Somewhere in that line was a person who would make him rich. Orlando's black eyes glittered at the thought.

Now it was time to get into costume. He planned on being in the lounge doing tricks, watching the passengers come aboard.

4

Chapter 2

All Aboard

Friday, June 26th 3 p.m.
Ensenada

"How much longer, Kim?" the little girl with blond corkscrew curls whined.

Soon. Look Stacie. People are starting to line up now."

Kim glanced around the large boarding area for the Sea Mystic, hoping to spot Mr. and Mrs. Gressner who had taken Julianna to the bathroom while Kim stayed with Stacie and Jason. As she looked at the two young children in her care, Kim felt a rush of gratitude that they still considered her their big sister. And she was even more grateful to the Gressners for suggesting that she go along on the cruise to help care for the kids.

She had been the Gressner's favorite babysitter until her junior year in high school. That was when Grant Gressner's Portland computer software firm split three ways, and he moved to Los Angeles to become owner and CEO of the L.A. portion. It had been nearly two years since she had seen the children. Shy, four year old Jason had only been two when they moved. Yet from the minute, Kim arrived Tuesday, he'd followed her around as if making up for lost time. As she helped eight year old Julianna, six year old Stacie, and four ("almost five" as he liked to remind her) year old Jason pack their bags, Kim's own excitement threatened to equal the feverish pitch of theirs. On the drive down to Ensenada where they would board the ship, Kim found herself counting off the miles with the children.

A cruise! It was something she had often dreamed of. True, she'd be plenty busy riding herd on the kids, but the idea of sailing some place on a luxurious ship was a delightful contrast to the studious year she had just finished at Oregon State University.

So here they were. One of the cruise line personnel announced that passengers bearing red boarding cards should line up now.

"That's us!" Stacie yelled.

Just then, Kim saw Mr. and Mrs. Gressner walking across the lobby with Julianna skipping happily between them.

"They just called us," Kim said.

"Okay, kids get your backpacks," Mrs. Gressner told them.

Even little Jason had a colorful nylon backpack stuffed with books and toys. Kim helped him put it on and then grabbed her own small sports bag. Their luggage would be brought to the cabins later. She felt a shiver of excitement as she thought of the royal blue silk dress her mother had bought her for the "Captain's Dinner."

Images of television shows and movies about exciting shipboard encounters and adventures flashed through her mind. But one look at the bouncing trio of blond children ahead of her quickly dispelled that notion.

"Dit dit dit dit   dit dit."

"Good, Jason. That's exactly right. Now you know both HI and SOS. As soon as you and your sisters learn all the letters, I'll teach you some fun games."

"I know all my letters. I learned them on Sesame Street."

"Oh, I know you know your letters. I mean learn them in Morse Code."

"Dit dit dit dit   dit dit"

Kim whirled around at the sound of "Hi" in code and faced a laughing nice-looking man behind her.

"Are you a ham radio operator?" he asked smiling.

"Yes — Kim Stafford, KA7SJP. And you are too?"

"Larry Reeves, KB7NJV. This is my wife, Jill KB7NJU, my daughter, Melanie, N7WXA, son, Steve, KB7PYH, and our youngest daughter, Jessica. She doesn't have a license...yet."

"Oh Dad, " Jessica protested.

"I know SOS too!" Jason piped in. "Dit dit dit, dah dah dah, dit dit dit."

"Good for you, young man," Larry said approvingly. "See Jessica."

Jessica grimaced.

Stacie interrupted the conversation, tugging urgently on Kim's sleeve.

"What's he doing, Kim?"

Kim peered around the long line of passengers at two men dressed in shipboard whites who were taking photos of each person passing through the doorway.

"I guess we're going to get our picture taken," Kim told her and then laughed as Stacie immediately began running her fingers through her curls, just slightly shorter than Julianna's. "Don't worry; you look beautiful."

"Mom says Stacie's going to grow up to be a movie star," Julianna laughed. "Always looking at herself in the mirror."

They were up to the photographers now. Mr. Gressner put Stacie up on his shoulder and Kim squeezed in next to Mrs. Gressner behind Jason and Julianna.

"Big smile now. Everyone say CRUISE!"

Laughing, they proceeded up the gangway. Kim turned to wave good-bye to the Reeves family.

"Did you bring your handheld?" Melanie asked.

"You bet — you?"

Kim grinned and half-pulled a notebook style computer out of her backpack.

"Even portable packet. I have a friend I want to talk to in Astoria, and I'm sure I won't be able to hit any of the local repeaters until we get close."

Melanie laughed.

"I'm impressed! You've got the ham bug even worse than our family. Say why don't we use 145.62 simplex on board?"

"Sounds good to me," Kim said as Jason tugged her to catch up with Stacie and Julianna who were staring at a pretty uniformed woman at the head of the gangplank.

"Welcome to the Sea Mystic," the woman said. The name tag on her navy blue blazer read 'Joyce Lillan, Assistant Cruise Director.'

"What is your cabin number?" she asked Mr. Gressner cordially.

"Regalia 113 and 114."

"That's up one deck and to your left. You can take either the stairs or the elevator."

Jason was already halfway up the stairs. Kim ran after him.

"Whoa, big guy. Remember the rules. We're going to all stick together."

"I want to see our rooms and the porthole. We will have a porthole, won't we?" he asked.

"I think we're going to have regular windows. At least that's what it looked like in the brochure," Kim told him. "And your parents' room has a glass door that leads to a balcony."

"I'd rather have a porthole," Jason pouted.

"May I help you?" a tall man with a British accent asked them as they reached the Regalia Deck and turned down a hallway. He leaned over to look at Mr. Gressner's boarding pass.

"Right down this way, sir." he said formally.

"Who's he?" Jason whispered to Kim.

"The steward, I think. Remember I've never been on a cruise either," Kim whispered back.

The man stood back at the open doors to 113 and 114.

"Your luggage should be arriving shortly. My

name's Moses, and I'll be your cabin steward. Let me know if there is anything you need."

Jason stared up at him solemnly, and Moses smiled and patted him on the head. He turned and walked down the hall to greet another family.

"He talks funny," Stacie said.

Mr. Gressner laughed.

"He has a British accent. He probably thinks we talk funny."

Jason and Julianna yelled to Kim from the adjoining cabin.

"Hey look, Kim — bunk beds!"

He was right. In contrast to the large queen size bed in Mr. and Mrs. Gressner's cabin 113, cabin 114 had four bunk beds. Kim's first reaction was how small the rooms were — not nearly as big as most motel rooms. And the bathroom! Why it reminded her of the one in her parents' camping trailer. Except that this one was luxurious. Thick, plush towels, and little white bottles of shampoo and lotion, all labeled with the navy blue lettering THE SEA MYSTIC.

Soft, romantic music floated through the cabins, and Kim suddenly thought of Marc. She felt her cheeks flush and confirmed the feeling by looking in the mirror. Sure enough, she was blushing. Her reaction startled her. She had met Marc KA7ITR through ham radio over a year ago. They'd had unbelievable adventures together. She knew that Marc considered her his girlfriend, and while Kim readily admitted that he was her best friend, she had really resisted the notion of being anyone's girlfriend — insisting to him and to herself that she was much too focused on her schoolwork to have a serious relationship with anyone.

And here she was blushing, finding herself looking forward to their meeting in Astoria where the ship would dock Monday night. Marc was part of the summer music festival there.

He'd had given her the good news that he was staying with parents of his friend, Bill, and the even better news that Bills' mother was a ham radio operator too. She was all set up on the local packet bulletin board, and since Kim had a portable packet with her via a notebook computer, they would be able to communicate at sea.

Then when the ship approached Astoria, they would talk to each other on the two meter band. Marc had said the music rehearsals wouldn't give him much spare time, but he promised to leave her a packet message on the Los Angeles Bulletin Board System twice a day.

Kim looked at the kids bouncing up and down on the beds. She was sure it would be quite a bit later tonight before she would have any time to try to send him a message. Her thoughts were interrupted by Jason's excited voice.

"Look Kim — a porthole!"

She couldn't help laughing at Jason's delight. To the left side of the room above the small dressing table area was a full length window, but above the top right-hand bunk which Jason now happily occupied was a small porthole.

"I bet they added it just for you," Kim teased.

"Let's go see the ship," Julianna whined.

Mrs. Gressner, standing in the doorway, looked at Kim questioning.

"Sure, no problem, Mrs. Gressner. You two get settled in, and I'll take the kids on a tour."

Leaving the Gressners to enjoy the bouquet of flowers just delivered from their travel agent, Kim herded the kids down the hallway.

"Dit dit dit dit dit dit," Jason yelled as he raced toward the stairs.

"Dit dit dit dah dah dah dah dit dah dah dit,"

"What?" Jason turned to Kim.

"That's stop."

"Oh."

"Let's go up," Kim suggested as she reached down to grab Jason's hand to keep him from racing ahead.

They climbed three levels of stairs, past the Promenade Deck, the Royalty Deck, the Bridge Deck, and finally out into the warm air of the Sun Deck.

"A swimming pool!" cried Julianna.

"And a slide!" Jason added.

Kim clutched their hands as they walked around the edge of the shipboard pool, three jacuzzis, rows and rows of lounge chairs, ping pong tables, and a mini basketball court.

"This is fun!" Stacie said, jumping up and down. "Can we go swimming now, Kim?"

"You don't think we'd be cold?"

Kim looked up at the typical for L.A. June cloud-covered skies.

"Naw, it's warm," Jason said kneeling by the pool and leaning over to trail his fingers through the water.

"Maybe later. Right now, let's go tour the rest of the ship."

The four of them walked down a flight of stairs at the stern of the ship and discovered themselves in the midst of an outdoor cafe. Three men, dressed in white, were busy setting out trays of cookies and little sandwiches. The children's eyes grew big at the array of goodies, and Stacie tugged on Kim's hand.

"I'm hungry.

"Would you like some of our teatime treats?" one of the men asked.

"Just a little," Kim said. "Your parents won't like it if I let you fill up on cookies. From what I've heard about cruises, we're going to have a wonderful dinner."

"I'll eat everything, I promise," Jason said, helping himself to four cookies and two sandwiches.

Kim quickly removed two of the cookies and one sandwich and put them on Julianna's plate.

"Seriously, you guys, that's enough. Here, we can get a glass of punch to wash this down."

They sat at one of the white metal tables by the railing and watched the stream of passengers still coming up the gangway. Within five minutes, the children were done eating, and Kim scurried to keep up with them as they ran down another stairwell onto the promenade deck.

"What are those lines for?" Jason asked, pointing at the deck.

"Shuffleboard," Kim said. "I've never played, but I've seen it on tv. You have a little flat thing you push with a stick. Maybe we can try it tomorrow."

They walked down the deck to the first set of heavy double doors leading inside. To their surprise, they were in a miniature shopping mall. A beauty shop, clothing store, drug store, and a tiny pizzeria all lined up side by side.

Stacie pressed her face to the glass of the small clothing boutique, admiring a white teddy bear dressed up in a tiny navy blue sweater with the Sea Mystic's logo on it.

They spent the next half hour wandering through the halls on various levels, peeking into the closed casino and theaters, examining books and games in the library and checking out the public bathrooms. Stacie was terrified of the loud flushing noise the shipboard toilets made and convinced Kim to let her get completely across the restroom before the toilet was flushed.

"Where's Jason?" Kim asked Julianna as she followed Stacie from the restroom.

"Over there," Julianna said, pointing toward a lounge. "He's watching a man."

"And I'm supposed to be watching Jason," Kim muttered under her breath as she walked the two girls toward the lounge.

Sure enough, Jason was sitting quietly in a chair watching a tall dark-haired man in a black suit do magic tricks. The man's oily dark hair glistened in the dim lounge light. He smiled at Kim as she sat down with the girls.

"Welcome children," he said in a low theatrical voice. "Come help Orlando do some tricks."

He flashed another smile at Kim, exposing crooked stained teeth. A creepy feeling shivered down her spine, but she smiled back and watched as the children sat entranced by his tricks.

Jason giggled when Orlando pulled a quarter from behind his own ear and then leaned over to find another behind Jason's.

The girls seemed amazed as the magician went through a repertoire of sleight of hand tricks. Feathers that turned into scarfs, scarfs that turned into rubber balls. Kim watched the man's intense black eyes focused on Jason and instinctively slipped her own arm around his small shoulders. There was something about magic that always made her feel a little uneasy.

Chapter 3

Bon Voyage!

Friday, June 26th 5:30 p.m.
Ensenada

I n the middle of a card trick, a huge blast of the ship's whistle sounded. Kim and the children jumped up in surprise. The magician kept on dealing cards calmly as though he hadn't heard anything.

"Uh oh, five thirty," Kim said softly. We're supposed to be back by now."

Orlando gathered up the cards.

"What is your name?" he asked Jason.

"Jason...", Jason said looking down at the floor. "I'm almost five."

"And these are your beautiful sisters?"

Jason giggled.

"Well, Jason , almost five, and beautiful sisters, be sure to come to my special magic shows for young people. There's one tomorrow night and an extra special show Monday night. I promise you that Orlando the Great will give you a performance you won't forget."

"Okay," Jason said, still looking down bashfully."

"We gotta go, Mr. Orlando. Thank you," Kim said. She led the children down the hallway, up the stairs, and through the long corridor to Regalia 114.

"There you are!" Mrs. Gressner exclaimed. "We're in the first dinner seating, so if you're going to get cleaned up and have any time left to see the ship sail, we have to hurry."

"Guess what, Mom? We met a real live magician," Jason said.

His loss for words over, he excitedly told her about the tricks Orlando had performed and about the upcoming shows.

"That's nice, dear," Mrs. Gressner said, combing his tousled hair. "We'll make sure you get to go. Now hurry and get ready for dinner."

"And the magician said we were all beautiful," Stacie giggled.

"Well now that's one very smart man," Mr. Gressner said.

****

"Dinner's just about ready," Ann Jensen KA7ITT told Marc as he tussled on the floor with their Border Collie, "Patches."

"It smells wonderful," Marc said as he sat down at the table. He was glad his friend, Bill, had convinced him to call his parents even though he'd been reluctant. "Your parents have never even met me," Marc had protested. "And besides, you'll be off in Montana at that firefighting job."

"Doesn't matter. They'll love having you. Fact is, my mom's happiest when she's cooking for college kids. Trust me. You'll like them and they'll like you."

Bill was right. They welcomed him immediately. And Bill, who loved surprises, purposefully didn't tell Marc that his mother was a ham radio operator. Apparently, he had a bet with his mother that it would take Marc less than thirty seconds to find that out.

"He wins," Ann said with a smile, as she opened the door to Marc who was standing, staring up at the three element beam mounted on the eaves of their upper story. "Bill said you'd know right away. I wasn't sure everyone scanned rooftops for antennas, so I took the bet. Silly me."

Together Jerry and Ann ran a large fuchsia greenhouse operation. It seemed to take most of their time, but Ann said she always found time for ham radio.

"And Patches," she said smiling at the black and white dog who sat listening to their table conversation as though she understood every word. "As a family, we trained a few guide dog puppies through 4H, but when the boys went off to college, I decided to get and train a dog of my own. A friend of mine has a dog she trained for disaster search and rescue. Patches loves to find people, so she seemed like a natural."

"And is she?" Marc asked.

"Oh yes," Ann said somewhat sadly. "Her first real test was the Oklahoma City tragedy. We flew there to help. It was quite a test emotionally for both of us."

Marc raised his eyes questioning.

"The search dogs got very depressed after the first few days. See we train them to find live humans. A person hides and the dog seeks him out and then the person praises the dog and gives it a food reward. So it's a fun, joyful activity for the dog. After all the live survivors were pulled out, there was nothing left but dead bodies. The dogs found them, but they were obviously sad."

Marc turned to look at Patches with new appreciation.

"In fact, at the advice of one of the trainers, every few hours, we would take the dogs to a park and set up a fake search with a live person to reinforce the idea that a search has a happy ending."

"So what's she done since then?"

"Lots. Last month, she found two lost children near Mt. Hood, and they were both very much alive," Ann said scratching the dog's ears who seemed to know she was being praised.

"Tell us about your studies," Jerry interrupted. "Ann will talk dogs to you all evening, if you let her."

"Oh Jerry, I won't either."

At that, Patches barked, and they all laughed. They ate and visited. Marc told them a little about his computer science studies at Oregon State University, and then he turned the topic to Kim and the planned arrival of the Sea Mystic in Astoria on Monday.

"So that was the girl you phoned last night to tell about Packet," Ann said smiling.

"My wife likes romances almost as much as she does dogs," Jerry winked at Marc.

****

Even with all their scurrying, the Gressners were a few minutes late to dinner. The maitre'd escorted them to their table. It was one of the few seating twelve in the dining room. Kim's eyes opened in surprise when she saw the other family already seated — the Reeves.

"Ham radio operators already believe in coincidence," Jill Reeves laughed.

Amy and Grant Gressner shook hands with the Reeves. Kim got the kids settled down and then sat down next to Melanie. She was pleased to have someone her own age to talk to. The kids were absorbed in watching the waiters expertly carrying heavy trays back and forth, so Kim turned to visit with her new friend.

Kim discovered that Melanie was a year younger than she was — just getting ready to start school at U.C.L.A. Like Kim, she'd had her Amateur Radio license for several years.

"You should get Kim to tell you some of the adventures she's had with that radio of hers," Grant Gressner said to Melanie.

"Really?" asked Melanie.

"Oh just some stuff," said Kim.

"Yeah stuff like rescuing a lost hiker, being kidnapped by bank robbers, getting stuck in a forest fire, and catching cocaine dealers."

Kim blushed at Mr. Gressner's speech.

"How'd you know all that?" she protested.

"Your parents sent a letter along with their anniversary picture. Said it would explain why they had more gray hair this year."

The waiter appeared to take their orders so Kim was saved from having to talk about herself. After dinner, on deck as she walked around with Melanie, some of the details came out. The two of them stood at the rail, the California sea breeze in their faces, as they watched the lights along shore grow more distant.

"Marc, right?" Melanie said, holding her two meter rig in her hand. "Most of the men I meet on the air are retired."

Kim laughed.

"It's getting better. The club at our school has grown from ten to forty-seven just in the year I've been there."

"You think we can hit the coastal repeaters from here?"

"Sure, I'd guess we're near L.A. now. Here let me check the frequencies."

Kim pulled the small repeater directory out of her purse. For the next hour, she and Melanie chatted with hams on the mainland. Two young ladies aboard a cruise ship definitely drew attention, and they had fun answering call after call. As one deep male voice came back, Melanie whispered to Kim.

"Whadya think?"

Kim shook her head.

"Nope, at least forty."

"How can you tell stuff like that?"

"Oh just lots of time on the air. I'm usually right but I have been fooled a few times."

The girls finally signed clear and wandered up to the sun deck where some couples were dancing to a small combo. Kim turned to Melanie.

"You know, I guess I'd better turn in. I told the

Gressners I'd be back by ten. They want to go to the late night show."

"Yeah and I bet the little ones are going to be rarin' to go at the crack of dawn. You know, I'd be happy to help you with them if you want."

"Really? Thanks Melanie. I'd like that a lot, but don't give up anything you want to do just to hang out with me."

"You mean like meeting Prince Charming?"

The girls both laughed at that and Kim turned to run down the stairs to their cabin.

"Did you have a good time?" Amy Gressner asked her as Kim tiptoed into the room.

"I did. It's really lovely up on deck this time of evening. I hope I didn't keep you waiting."

"Not at all. Grant's just getting his necktie on now. The kids are sound asleep. They were really tired."

"Me too," yawned Kim.

She told the Gressners goodnight and then slipped into the cabin with the children. The moonlight through the porthole was ample for her to operate her computer and radio. Sure enough, Marc had left a message for her on the Los Angeles bulletin board. He was staying with some friends, rehearsals were going well, and most of all, he was looking forward to seeing her Monday night.

"Me too," Kim wrote back.

****

Kim lay in bed wide awake until after midnight, partly because her head was full of thoughts and partly because her stomach was full of food. She just wasn't used to going to bed feeling so stuffed. The five course meal of fruit cocktail, clam chowder, garden salad, Teriyaki chicken, and chocolate cake had been wonderful. Everyone at the table had ordered something different, and she smiled when she thought of Jason's face when all the desserts arrived.

But the next morning at 6 a.m., she was awake and hungry. Hungry? How could it be?

I've probably already stretched my stomach — bet I'll weigh 300 pounds by Monday, she thought, turning over to look out the window. A beautiful California sunrise was just beginning.

The kids were still sleeping soundly. Unless they had changed their habits dramatically in the last two years, Kim knew none of them would wake before seven and only then grudging. Quietly, she slid out of bed and dressed in the dim dawn light.

"Well you don't look any fatter yet," she told herself in the mirror as she hurriedly combed her hair and put on light makeup.

Satisfied that the children weren't stirring, Kim slipped a key into the pocket of her green sweatshirt and closed the door behind her quietly.

"Good morning, Ma'am," Moses greeted her.

"You're up too?" Kim questioned, laughing.

"Oh yes, Ma'am, there's lots to be done early in the morning."

And indeed there was. As Kim climbed the stairs to the observation deck, she passed dozens of crew members mopping floors, polishing banisters, and dusting furniture. She pushed open the heavy double doors and stepped out onto the varnished wooden deck. Several passengers were already out walking the promenade circle around the ship.

She looked to see if by chance any of the Reeves family had made it up yet. When she didn't see them, she transmitted on simplex on her handheld. If Melanie was like Kim, she would turn the rig on first thing in the morning and monitor as she got dressed. No answer. Oh well, she knew the rest of the world didn't rise at dawn like she did... but she often wondered why not. It was the best time of the day.

Kim admired the breaking sunrise as she joined the line of passengers walking the ship's circumference. Ocean spray and early morning dew made the deck slippery, and Kim was grateful for her rubber-soled shoes as she made her way toward the stern of the ship. Sure enough, the outdoor cafe was in full swing. The smell of hot steaming coffee and freshly baked breakfast delicacies greeted her.

I'll just have one little roll and some hot chocolate, she told herself, but when she was through the serving line, her plate was heaped with fresh fruit, croissants, and bagels. She found a place sheltered from the breeze and sat down to enjoy the morning sun reflecting off the ocean.

In the middle of the night, they would dock in San Francisco and tomorrow they would explore the city. The Gressners had promised the kids they would go to China Town and ride on the cable cars — both experiences Kim had never had either.

Kim smiled at the white-haired couple sitting at the next table, as she tried to absorb her surroundings into her memory bank. They were sitting side by side holding hands. Were they newlyweds or had it always been like that for them? What did it take to make a love stay strong for a lifetime? Kim was watching them, thinking romantic thoughts when a voice interrupted her.

"Well, we meet again, beautiful lady."

Kim looked up, startled.

Orlando, dressed in jeans and a faded sweatshirt was standing by her table.

Chapter 4

Treasure Hunt

Saturday, June 16th 6:30 a.m.
At sea

"Mind if I join you?

"No, I mean uh, sure, go ahead," Kim stammered, feeling a warm flush of embarrassment.

Orlando sat down, cradling a hot cup of coffee in his hands. He was smoking a cigarette and Kim moved her head to avoid the drifting smoke. She studied his face intently. In the morning light, dressed in ordinary clothes, he didn't looks as sinister, but still she didn't find him at all appealing. He smiled, showing his discolored teeth.

"First cruise?" he asked.

"Yes."

"Where are your sisters and brothers?"

"Well actually, they're not. I mean I'm just their babysitter. Their parents brought me along to take care of them. They're still sleeping."

"Ah, I see," Orlando said. " So you've gotten up to have a few minutes to yourself before your motherly duties start."

"I guess you could put it that way. But, I need to get back because they'll be getting up for breakfast and then I think we'll be doing a treasure hunt or something."

Kim looked at her watch. Seven o'clock. She hadn't touched the food on her plate.

"Well, I guess I have to go," she said, standing up abruptly.

Orlando looked at her full plate questioningly.

"Yeah, I know. I thought I was hungry but I guess not," Kim said feeling herself blush again. "I really have to get back."

Orlando smiled again almost as if he enjoyed Kim's awkwardness.

"Well make sure you bring the children to my special magic show this evening. I guarantee they'll like it. And at the Monday show I'll do the disappearing act."

"Okay, I will. Thanks, Mr. Orlando. Gotta go.

Kim excused herself from the table and put her full plate onto one of the busboy trays. Why did she feel so flustered around the magician? She'd behaved like an absolute dork. He was only trying to be polite. Just something about him, she guessed. She glanced over her shoulder as she left and saw Orlando sitting down at another table with a family of three little girls. He said something and they laughed.

Kim closed the heavy cafe door behind her and hurried along the deck. The morning sun, now in full bloom, felt good. She went inside the ship and ran down the carpeted stairs to Regalia deck.

Just as she thought, the children were just waking up. Kim had picked up a couple of bulletins announcing the day's agenda, and she handed one to Julianna.

Julianna read the words aloud slowly for the others.

"Treasure Hunt at 9 a.m. Oh, can we do that?"

"You bet. I like treasure hunts, too. We better get you guys down to breakfast so you'll have energy for all this."

Julianna was still poring over the activity sheet.

"Pizza at three in the ship's cafe. Can we do that, too, Kim? I love pizza."

Kim laughed and patted the girl's small stomach.

"We're both going to be tugboats, Julianna, if we eat everything they offer."

Julianna didn't hear her as she was busy reading the next item.

"Children's magic show at 7:30 p.m. Oh, I bet that's with Mr. Orlando!" she said excitedly.

"I bet so too," Kim said. "As a matter of fact, I just saw him up in the cafe drinking coffee. He gave us a special invitation to the show. Said something about a disappearing act."

"Neat," Jason said sleepily.

Jason had picked up "neat" from his father, and the whole family laughed every time he said it.

"Right now, you'd better disappear into the bathroom and get ready for breakfast," Kim said.

The three children struggled into their clothes and with some supervision from Kim got their faces washed and hair combed.

"Well talk about perfect timing. Look at you all ready to go," Mr. Gressner said from the doorway.

Mrs. Gressner flashed a smile of approval at Kim.

"Having fun?" she asked her as they all walked behind the kids on the way to the dining room.

"Yes, I am, Mrs. Gressner."

Mrs. Gressner interrupted her.

"Kim, if you don't feel uncomfortable doing it, I wish you'd call us Amy and Grant. I know you're just being respectful like your parents taught you to be, but you're an adult now... and oh I don't know, it just makes me feel old."

"I'd be pleased to, Mrs... oops, I mean Amy."

"Now go on with what you were saying. I interrupted you."

"Well I've walked all over this ship, and I still don't think I've seen everything. And the people... I hear all sorts of languages. I wonder where everyone is from?"

"Ask them, Kim. It's a good way to start a conversation."

She laughed as she said that and then half-apologized. "Not that I have to tell you anything about communicating. I've heard you talking on that radio of yours. Was it just naturally easy for you to talk to strangers or did it take it awhile?"

"Oh, I guess I was kind of shy at first, but you know I've discovered there really aren't any strangers in the world, just people you haven't met. I guess that's sounds trite, but it's true."

Amy Gressner put her arm around Kim affectionately.

"You're doing a great job with the kids, Kim. You don't how much Grant and I appreciate having you along."

There was little time to bask in the compliment as the waiter led them to their table. Kim was wondering where the Reeves were when they came scooting in just behind them.

"I called you on the radio," Kim told Melanie, "but I don't think you were up."

"No," laughed Melanie. "In fact, I wasn't up until about five minutes ago. I don't know why I'm so tired — all that food, I guess."

"Well here we go again," Kim said, glancing at the menu.

All her favorites: pancakes, waffles, French toast, Eggs Benedict. She frowned trying to make a decision.

Mrs. Gressner ordered for the children. One waiter brought them freshly-squeezed orange juice while another passed plates of pastries. Kim thought of the ones she had left untouched in the cafe and took a jelly-filled croissant.

Wasteful, she scolded herself mentally. But she found that very little of the breakfast was wasted when it arrived. She managed to eat all of her Eggs Benedict and pancakes and drink a second glass of orange juice.

The waiter, a slim young man with light blond hair hovered over their table.

"How about some more juice, young man?"

"No thank you, Mr.?"

"You can just call me, Ferdy. What's your name?"

"Jason. Jason Gressner, and I can spell it too. J...A...S...O...N. I'm almost five."

"Well good for you, Jason. You're a smart young man."

****

Orlando lay down on his bunk and smoked another cigarette. There really wasn't much to do. He'd made the contacts he needed to. Now it was just a matter of waiting.

And after all his years of prison time, waiting was something he was very good at.

****

"KA7ITR from AA7RW"

"AA7RW from KA7ITR. Good morning, Lynn. How are you?"

"Fine, Marc. What time do you plan to be there for setup this afternoon?"

"Actually, I'm dropping my bass off now before I do a little tourist stuff. Performance is at two — I'd guess we all ought to be there around one. What are you up to this morning?"

"Taking the kids berry picking before the rain rots them all. Incidentally I wanted to tell you that I really enjoyed your playing last night. You certainly know your way around a bass. I'm glad we got hold of you. By the way, I bet you're enjoying your stay with the Jensens."

"Absolutely. Parents of one my friends and he didn't even bother to tell me his mother was a ham. This whole week is a nice break before I start my construction job with my uncle. Score another one for ham radio. If I hadn't met you at the Seaside Convention, I'd have never heard about the jazz festival in Astoria."

"A lucky coincidence for everyone concerned, Marc. We didn't know our bass player wouldn't be able to make it until the day before I left for Seaside."

"That isn't end of the twists of fate, Lynn. A good

friend of mine — also a ham radio operator — is on the cruise ship that's making Astoria part of its inaugural cruise. She'll be here Monday night in time for our performance."

"That's great, Marc. Listen, the kids are ready. I need to run. I'll see you this afternoon."

"Good Lynn, I'll look forward to it. Have fun in the berry fields. AA7RW from KA7ITR, clear and monitoring."

Marc smiled as he drove down the quiet streets of Astoria. Red, white, and blue flags with the bright logo "The Magic of Astoria" fluttered from every lamp post. Festival excitement had transformed every corner of the fishing port town. Every store owner in town was cashing in on the magic theme. "No sleight of hand here," "Illusions of Beauty," "Pick a car, any car," were just a few of the signs he saw as he drove south on Marine Drive toward the Columbia River Maritime Museum.

He parked his truck and hesitated a minute, trying to decide whether to explore the museum itself or the docked "Columbia," the last seagoing lighthouse to serve on the U.S. West Coast. He decided on the lightship and joined the tourists lining up to board.

At the mouth of the Columbia River, Astoria was full of maritime history — everything from eighteenth century river explorers to steamboats to the famed Japanese shelling of Fort Stevens during World War II. And then of course, there were stories about the Shanghai days in which unsuspecting drunk saloon patrons were dropped through trap doors into waiting rowboats underneath that would take them to waiting ships for forced servitude. Astoria had once been built on wooden piers so it was possible for small boats to maneuver right under the town.

Marc walked up the gangplank, eager to sail back in time.

****

After breakfast, Mr. and Mrs. Gressner returned to the cabin while Kim took the kids to the main lobby to line up for the treasure hunt. Miss Lillan was there — this time in white shorts and a royal blue t-shirt. She handed out lists and pencils to all the children.

Kim smiled at Melanie who was standing with Jessica as Miss Lillan explained the rules.

"There are ten items on the list. All of the items are in public hallways. In other words, don't try going in the kitchens or anywhere else that says 'Crew Only.' When you find an item, look at the orange letter that will be on it somewhere. Write it down on your list. First one back here with the completed list wins the grand prize. But don't feel bad if you're not first. We have prizes for everyone."

With a loud cheer, the kids were on their way. Kim glanced down the list. First item: Statue of Queen Elizabeth.

"I've got an idea," she told the children. "Everyone will be running in a pack looking for the first item. Why don't we start at the bottom of the list? That way if we find an item, the rest of them won't see where it is."

"Yeah!" said Julianna.

"Neat!" yelled Jason.

Stacie jumped up and down, her curls bobbing.

"Okay, number ten is biggest pie plate on board," Julianna read. "I thought we weren't supposed to go in the kitchen."

"How about pizza pie?" Kim suggested.

They were off and running down the hallway toward the pizzeria in the little mall. They giggled and hushed themselves from cheering when they found the orange letter "Z" on the edge of a huge pizza tin on the wall. Then they were off to find number nine — "opposite of death ship."

The kids looked at her puzzled.

"What's another word for ship?" Kim asked them.

"Boat?" Julianna said.

"Right — and what's the opposite of death?"

"Alive? Life?"

The kids beat her to the stairs that led to Promenade Deck where a row of lifeboats was on each side.

"Okay, you girls check these, and Jason and I will check the ones over there — Jason? Jason?"

Kim whirled around looking for him.

"He was right behind us," Stacie said. "I passed him on the stairs when he stopped to pick up a bug."

Kim felt her heart pounding as she raced back to the stairwell.

"KA7SJP from N7WXA."

Kim grabbed her two meter rig from her pocket.

"Not now, Melanie. We're looking for Jason."

"He's right here with us. We found him wandering around on the Main Deck."

Kim felt like crumpling to the deck with relief.

"Oh thank God. Where are you? I'll be right there."

"Right outside the door leading to the Illusions Lounge."

Grabbing each girl by a hand, Kim ran down the stairs. Jason was sitting with Melanie on a bench.

"Oh, Jason — I'm sorry — I thought you were right with us."

"I was looking for Mr. Orlando. When does he do the magic tricks again?"

Kim forcibly quieted her breathing. Here she was nearly hysterical and Jason himself was as calm as could be. Still, she didn't plan to let him out of her sight ever again.

"Tonight — sometime after dinner. Oh Melanie, I'm sorry. We took you out of the treasure hunt. Jessica probably hates us — where is she anyway?"

"Over there," Melanie said pointing to a group of kids having their faces painted by a clown. "We just about got trampled looking for the first clue, and she decided it wasn't too much fun."

"Yeah — that's why we were doing them in reverse order. Oh well, I guess there'll be another one later in the week."

"It's all your fault, Jason," Stacie accused.

"Is not."

"Is too."

"What is?"

He looked so innocent and questioning that they all burst out laughing, even Stacie.

"I've got an idea," said Kim. "Let's get our faces painted."

"Even you?" asked Julianna.

"Even me."

The morning flew by for the children and Kim. She even managed to fit in a little code practice with them — this after they watched her and Melanie make several contacts with stations on shore. Jessica Reeves said that she might like to learn the code too so for about fifteen minutes, the group, all painted like clowns, sat in the sunshine and played a guessing game.

Kim was amazed at Jason's ability to absorb the code. Four years old ("almost five" she smiled) and he already had several letters down pat. At this rate, she thought, he'll have his license by the time he is five.

Amy Gressner came to tell the group it was time for lunch. She laughed when she saw their faces and didn't object when the children voted to keep their clown makeup on through the meal.

After feasting on the elaborate buffet luncheon (in which Jason managed to eat four desserts) Kim took the children to the cabin.

"I'm not sleepy," protested Stacie even though she yawned as she said it.

"Mom says if we want to stay up for the magic show tonight, we have to take a rest," Julianna lectured her.

"And Mr. Orlando told me to make sure and bring everyone tonight."

"Mr. Orlando? When did you see him?" Kim asked.

"This morning when we were standing in line to get our faces painted. You were talking to Melanie, and I was behind you. He came up right behind me and whispered in my ear, 'Bring your family to the magic show tonight.' I turned around and he was gone — or almost gone. I saw the tail of his black coat going around the corner. He really is magic, isn't he?"

"I wonder what tricks he'll do tonight? We can go, can't we Kim?" Jason pleaded.

"Sure, but remember your mom said you need to take a nap. So put some magic dust in your eyes and go to sleep. I'm ready for a nap too," Kim said, yawning.

Chapter 5

"The Amazing Orlando"

Saturday, June 16th 3 p.m.
At sea

"Bingo!" declared Ferdy in a low whisper. He leaned back against the bunk in Orlando's small cabin, being careful not to crease his freshly-ironed waiter's uniform.

"I've got three possibles for you, one at each of my tables. The Green family at Table 10. Talk about rich. You should see the diamonds on that woman's fingers — big enough to choke a horse. Two little boys dressed in designer clothes.

"Then there's the Hodkins at Table 11. They've got a girl about seven. You wouldn't know they were especially well off from the way they dress, but I overheard the Missus say this is their fifteenth cruise."

"And at Table 12, there's the Gressner family of six. All I know about them is that the man has had to leave the table a couple of times to make phone calls to his company."

"Really?"

Orlando's eyes gleamed with interest.

"I think I've met the kids, and their babysitter. I don't think she likes me much. I sat down with her at breakfast, and she scooted away like I was a snake or something."

"That could be bad," Ferdy said, shaking his head. "You don't think she suspects anything, do you?"

"What's there to suspect? She's just an inexperienced little brat who doesn't respect the attentions of a handsome gentleman like myself."

Ferdy snorted.

"Okay, so what do you want me to do besides talk up your show at dinner?"

"Nothing much. Tonight's really just a trial run. I think I'll target the Gressner's boy. If he doesn't work out, we'll pick someone else tomorrow for the real thing."

"You got the stuff to give him?"

"Yeah tucked away safe."

"Is Mitch ready in Astoria?"

"How do you know about Mitch?"

"You mentioned him. Remember the first time we talked about this whole deal a month ago?"

"Well you forget about Mitch, or anyone else I've talked about. All you need to know is what you're to do on this end. Understood?"

Ferdy didn't answer. Orlando looked at him appraisingly and continued talking.

"Look Ferdy, your biggest job will be after this thing is over. Everybody is going to have tons of questions at breakfast. You need to act as shocked as everyone else. Why, that poor little child. Such a cute innocent thing. A tear or two wouldn't hurt."

"I'll leave the acting to you, Leo."

"Orlando — I am Orlando — you'd better remember that all the time or else I may remember some things I saw in an alley one night."

A flush of red rose up Ferdy's neck, but he didn't say any more.

****

As promised, Ferdy promoted the magic show at dinner. The Green family said they wouldn't miss it for anything.

Their two boys, Tony and Chris grinned and nodded an enthusiastic yes. The Hodkins said maybe. Their daughter wasn't feeling too well — upset stomach.

Ferdy murmured sympathetically and brought her a large glass of 7 Up with a tiny pink parasol clinging to the rim of the frosty glass. She smiled and said maybe she felt better. Ferdy moved on to the Gressner's table to serve dessert.

"Haven't seen Orlando's show myself, but I've heard others say he's pretty good. Kids would probably enjoy it," Ferdy told Mrs. Gressner.

"Tonight and then Monday night too, right?" Mr. Gressner asked.

"I've seen him do tricks — lots of tricks," Jason offered.

"Well good for you. Maybe he'll teach you some," Ferdy said as he looked at the Gressner children with their light blond hair, the color of his own. The little boy looked kind of like his nephew. He grabbed the heavy stack of used plates and walked back to the kitchen. He'd be glad when this cruise was over.

****

"I think I'll just lie here for a little while before I get dressed," Mrs. Gressner said to Kim back in the cabin.

Kim looked at the green silk dress hanging on the open closet door. It was made of sheer fabric almost chiffon-like in texture, and Kim imagined Mrs. Gressner would look beautiful floating around on the dance floor. She wished for a moment that she could watch the dance, but Stacie was tugging at her elbow.

"Put a ribbon in my hair, Kim, please."

Patiently, Kim brushed her golden curls and tied a red polka dot ribbon at the crown of Stacie's head. In her red and white corduroy overalls, Stacie looked adorable. She stood on her tiptoes to admire herself in the mirror.

"Okay, Stace... that's enough."

Kim set her on the bunk to wait while Julianna and Jason finished getting ready. Mr. Gressner handed her the camera.

"See if you can get a photo to put in a scrapbook. Amy and I will stop by on our way to the dance if you're not back yet."

The kids hugged their parents good-bye, and Kim opened the door to the hallway, trying hard to stifle a yawn. She hadn't been able to fall asleep this afternoon and now she felt really tired. Amazing how the young ones were fully charged with energy. I must be getting old at nineteen, Kim thought.

They scurried across the open promenade deck, stopping for a moment to admire the shore lights in the distance. When they woke up in the morning, they'd be in San Francisco, and they'd have all day to see the sights.

"Come on, let's go, " Jason begged. "Mr. Orlando may be doing tricks already."

Kim allowed the kids to pull her away from the rail and up the stairs to the main deck. Several families with small children were heading down the hall toward the Count's Lounge.

"Hurry," Jason urged. "All the best seats will be gone."

They entered the lounge where fifty chairs were set up around a small stage. Red velvet curtains blocked their view, but Kim could hear scurrying movements of people dragging furniture back and forth. "Orlando the Great" proclaimed bold silver letters on an easel in front of the curtain.

Jason pouted. The first two rows were all full.

"I told you so," he said, his eyes brimming with tears.

Just then, Miss Lillan stepped out on stage from between the curtains.

"Could we have all the adults sit in the back rows so that the children may see better, please."

Reluctantly, adults gave up their seats as children quickly filled them. Jason, Stacie, and Julianna made a beeline for the front row. Kim moved to the back.

After everyone had settled into seats, Miss Lillan made announcements about activities that would be available Sunday in San Francisco and a little about the Captain's dinner Sunday night. Just as the children began to stir restlessly in their seats, she gave a dramatic pause.

"And now, Ladies and Gentlemen for your magical pleasure, in his first performance aboard the Sea Mystic, I present the great, the one and only master of magic, Orlando!"

Kim sat on the edge of her chair trying to see the children's reaction. Jessica turned and gave her a quick smile as Orlando stepped out on stage to applause.

In his black long-tailed tux and tall hat under the glow of stage lights, Orlando appeared even more imposing than he had in the lounge the afternoon before. Something about the way he looked out over his audience made Kim's stomach flutter anxiously. She sat on her hands and tried to relax.

The magician moved swiftly through his routine. A stuffed bunny appeared from his hat; a playing card signed by a girl in the front row was torn in half and set afire and yet mysteriously reappeared in the girl's pocket.

There was even one trick that didn't work — a crystal ball supposed to be suspended in mid-air, crashed to the ground, dashing slivers across the stage. Orlando laughed and made a joke as though he had intended for the trick to fail. But Kim saw the dark flush of anger on his face, and she noticed he didn't try it again.

However, a succession of swirling flags plucked from his collar and given to the children had them all clapping. "And now, for a special trick — one I learned from Sir William Roderick, master magician of England."

Kim had never heard of Sir Roderick, but no matter; Orlando sounded convincing enough.

I need a volunteer to help me for this special, special trick. Who would like to be sawed in half?"

There were gasps and giggles from the audience but then twenty hands waved wildly in the air. Kim looked to see if the Gressner children were among them. Julianna had hers up halfway. Stacie and Jason looked shyly at the floor. Orlando gazed out over the audience, fixing his stare on two boys in the front row that Kim recognized from the table next to theirs in the dining room. He closed his eyes and waved his right arm back and forth again across the sea of children.

"I choose... I choose... " he said, his eyes still closed.

Kim noticed that Jason had finally put his hand up. She held her breath not knowing whether to hope that he might be chosen or not.

"I choose you!" Orlando said, opening his eyes.

He was pointing at a ten year old boy sitting in the second row. Even from the back of the room, Kim could see Jason's shoulders sag. Her heart went out to him and yet there was a small part of her which felt relieved that all of the Gressner children had been passed over.

"I choose you!" the magician said again as the selected helper seemed frozen in his seat. With the urging of his seatmates, he got up and made his way to the stage.

Orlando looked down at the boy and whispered something to him. The boy whispered back.

"Ladies and Gentlemen, allow me to introduce my assistant ,Darren from Culver City."

With a prompt from Orlando, the boy took a bow and his family cheered. There was some quiet discussion between Orlando and Darren and the audience stilled, trying to hear what they were saying. Orlando turned back to the audience and smiled.

"Are you ready?"

"Yes!" they chorused.

"Good, now to make this happen, we all have to say the magic word 'Abracadabra' together. Let's practice it — okay?"

Obediently, the group said 'Abracadabra' several times, each one louder than the last until they were practically shouting.

"What's happening?"

Kim turned to find Mr. and Mrs. Gressner sitting down beside her in the back row. Mrs. Gressner looked lovely in the sheer green dress, and Mr. Gressner handsome in his dark blue suit. The mingled aroma of her light perfume and his after shave lotion made Kim long once again to be going to a dance instead of babysitting.

"He's just about to saw that little boy in half. I know Julianna and Jason wish they had been picked."

"Ooh," Mrs. Gressner said as she peered down the rows. Jason was slumped down in his seat, just the top of his blond head showing. "I don't like the looks of that saw. I'm happy for the kids just to watch this one."

"By the way, you look beautiful," Kim whispered.

Mrs. Gressner patted her hand. Orlando was getting things ready. He and Darren wheeled out a long red box with a gold stripe down the middle. Orlando whispered in his ear and Darren climbed in the box. His smiling face stuck out one end and his tennis-shoe clad feet wiggled out the other.

Orlando brandished a saw over his head and swung it around for the audience to see. Kim felt vaguely ill, but Darren was still smiling. Then Orlando put a cloth over the entire box and waved his hand across the middle several times.

Darren grimaced as the saw was placed against the wood and Orlando began rapid sawing motions. It seemed to take an awfully long time and the audience was clearly getting bored. Darren's eyes were wide, but he smiled gamely through it all. Finally the box was split in two and the bright red cloth was in shreds where it had been hacked through.

With a flourish, Orlando pulled up the far end of the cloth. Sure enough there were two tennis-shoed feet still wiggling. The audience cheered and Darren grinned. Then Orlando pushed the two sections back together and muttered some incantations over the split center.

"Are you okay?" he said to Darren.

"Yes!" was his enthusiastic reply.

Orlando opened the top near Darren's shoulders and helped to pull the young boy out who was obviously still intact and none the worse for his cutting adventure.

"Reeboks," whispered Mr. Gressner.

"What?" Kim whispered back.

"The kid's got on Reeboks — the feet sticking out the other end were wearing Nikes — I saw the swoosh trademark."

"Oh Grant — don't spoil it."

Orlando had come down into the audience now. He was doing small tricks: disappearing coins, water changing into dust, rope that appeared to be cut but which magically rejoined itself. The magician stopped at the row where the Gressner children were and bent over Jason, talking to him. Kim watched the little boy as his cheeks flushed and he nodded. Orlando handed him a small box which Jason held in front of him gingerly as he walked to the front of the stage. Grimacing, he held the box, which was now beginning to bulge, straight out before him.

Suddenly with a loud pop, the box exploded and red and white confetti rained down on the front row of delighted children. Jason scurried back to Orlando's side. Orlando tossed him a round ball which magically transformed into a box. At Orlando's urging, Jason opened the lid just as the stage lights zoomed in on him.

Jason squealed with delight as a small white rat emerged from the box and ran up his arm. Orlando plucked it from Jason's shoulder and put it back in the box. He closed the lid and had Jason open it again. Jason's mouth dropped open — at Orlando's urging he carried the empty box to the front of the stage to show to the audience. Orlando came up behind him and grabbed the white rat from the back of Jason's collar. Jason seemed very surprised to see the small creature again and for one comical moment the two of them stared at each other, nose to nose.

The kids applauded loudly and Miss Lillan spoke above their approval "Ladies and Gentlemen — the Amazing Orlando!"

Orlando came to center stage, took a bow, and then spoke.

"Thank you all for coming. You've been an especially good audience. I hope you'll all come back Monday night for an even bigger show. For the first time ever since I left England, I'm going to attempt the disappearing act."

"He doesn't sound very British to me."

"Grant, I think it's time we went to the dance. Obviously you've lost the magic of being a young believer."

Grant Gressner winked at Kim as his wife dragged him out the door. Kim laughed and went down to the edge of the stage where most of the children including her three charges were gathered around Orlando as he talked to the kids.

"On Monday, not only will I disappear from the stage, but I and an assistant will make the trip together. We will reappear right in the center aisle."

Fifty heads turned to look at the center aisle. Jason looked at Orlando. Kim looked at Jason who seemed in complete awe of the tall man beside him.

Orlando began gathering up his props as kids clamored to be his assistant for the next show.

"I will need many assistants for my tricks on Monday," he promised them. "I'll choose them at the beginning of the show so make sure you're all here."

He turned with a flourish and half bowed to Jason. Jason just stared at him with his mouth open.

"Thank you, Jason Gressner, for your excellent help," he said as he extended his hand. Jason took his hand solemnly, never taking his eyes off the magician's face.

Chapter 6

Code and Cruising

Saturday, June 16th 8:30 p.m.
At sea

Julianna and Stacie looked at their little brot.her with new respect as they left the lounge.

"He really is magic," Jason told them. "He knew my last name."

"What?" Kim asked.

"He called me Jason Gressner."

"Didn't he ask you what your name was when you went up on stage?"

"No," Jason said with almost adult clarity. "He asked that other boy, Darren, but he didn't ask me."

"Oh, he probably heard it somewhere," Kim told him, but that uneasy feeling she'd had when she'd first met Orlando came back to her. Oh well, Jason had done his bit on stage — maybe they wouldn't even go to the Monday night performance. She really would like to get off the ship at the first opportunity to see Marc.

"Let's go get some pizza," Stacie said as they passed the pizzeria on the Main deck.

Julianna groaned.

"Oooh, how could you eat anything else?"

Kim looked at each of the kids. Jason was quiet, absorbed in thought. Her stomach agreed with Julianna's.

"Why don't we go back to the cabin and watch TV or play a game for awhile? It's almost nine and we're going to have a full day tomorrow in San Francisco. Besides, I'd like to talk to Marc."

They'd heard about Marc but had never met him.

"How?" Julianna questioned. "I thought you said

you couldn't reach him with your radio until we got real close to where he is."

"That's true, but remember the little computer I brought along? I can talk to him on that — in fact, I did it last night after you all were asleep. He's looking forward to meeting all of you. Would you like to type a message to him too?"

That was enough incentive for the kids to go to the cabin although Stacie said she's rather play games on Kim's computer than talk to anyone.

"Dit dit dit dit dit dit," said Jason. "Are we going to talk to him with dits and dahs?"

Kim laughed.

"No, we're going to type a letter to him."

The kids watched eagerly as Kim attached something called a TNC to both her radio and the computer. She explained that the signal on the radio could hook them up to a place called a bulletin board where lots of people left messages for each other.

"How do they leave messages?" Stacie asked.

"They send them by radio."

The kids looked disbelieving but they sat down beside her as Kim typed in the commands that would connect her with the Los Angeles BBS where Marc had left her a message. Sure enough, information came back that there was mail for her from Marc Lawrence KA7ITR.

"See, he made a mailbox for me so he could leave a message."

"Mailbox? I don't see any mailbox," Jason said.

"It's a place in the system for messages."

She brought up the message on the screen and Julianna read it aloud.

"To Kim KA7SJP from Marc KA7ITR. Great talking to you last night. I am looking forward to seeing you and meeting the Gressners on Monday. Our reh..."

"Rehearsals," Kim prompted.

"Rehearsals are going well and the show should be good. Did I tell you that I have met two other hams in town?"

Julianna was tired of reading, so Kim continued.

"One of them, Lynn, is in the band, and I'm staying at the house of the other one. "Ann" trains search dogs for disasters. And get this... she must have gotten her license the same day I did because her call is just one letter off of mine —KA7ITT. By the way, Kim, lest you be jealous, not only is she married, she's old enough to be my mother. In fact she's Bill Jensen's mother at OSU. I'm not sure if you ever met him. He was in my physics lab and we used to do our reports together."

Kim laughed. She had never ever said anything about being jealous to Marc, yet deep down she kind of liked the fact that he was reassuring her. Another feeling she hadn't quite dealt with in herself. Hmmm. This cruise was making her think in ways she hadn't before. She typed rapidly.

"Hi Marc! Yes, I got your message. We are looking forward to seeing you too. We all plan to come to the concert. There will be a magic show for kids here on board just after we dock. I'm not absolutely sure the kids want to go to it, but I kind of think they do. So as soon as that's over, we'll be down to the town center. I believe you said you were performing most of the afternoon and all evening — right? What time is it all over? Hope we can have some time together, afterwards. 88's Kim."

"What's 88's?" Julianna asked.

"Never mind," said Kim.

"I know," Stacie said full of self-importance. "It's a card game."

"I think that's crazy 8's," Kim laughed.

"Oh yeah," Stacie said. "Can you show us how to play? I've got a deck of cards."

"Only if all of you can get into your pajamas and get your teeth brushed by the time I count to 88."

****

Sunday, June 17th
San Francisco

"Wake up, Kim," Stacie insisted as she shook her shoulder.

Kim pulled a pillow over her face and groaned. Bad mistake. All three kids were on her, pulling the pillow away and tickling her. With a huge growl, she sat up and grabbed them, pretending to be a wild beast about to dine on young children. Their squeals of delight prompted her to hush them.

"Shhh you guys — your parents are still asleep."

"No, they're not," Julianna said. "I just heard the shower start in their bathroom."

As if to confirm her statement, the door between the two rooms opened and Mrs. Gressner, clad in a white terry cloth robe, poked her head in.

"I thought I heard a lion in here?"

"Oh Mom, that was just Kim," Jason said.

Kim smiled and self consciously ran her fingers through her tangled hair.

"Did you have fun at the dance?" she asked.

"We did although I'm afraid Grant and I have gotten a little rusty. I don't want to think how many years it's been since we went out dancing. To tell the truth, we folded about midnight and came back to bed."

"So that's why you're up early."

"That and San Francisco. You've never been here, have you, Kim?"

"No."

"You're in for a treat. Let's get the kids going. Maybe this afternoon, Grant will watch them for awhile and you and I can go shopping."

"I'd like that."

"I wanna go shopping too," Stacie said.

"You will," her mother assured her. "First stop is China Town. Remember the five dollars your grandmother gave each of you? You'll find all sorts of fun stuff to buy in the shops. Although, I suppose the things that were five and ten cents back when I was a kid are now a dollar or two."

"You sound like my parents," Kim laughed. "Always talking about the good old days when ice cream cones were a nickel."

"Can I have ice cream for breakfast, Kim?" Jason asked.

"Ooomh, we'll see. How about pancakes or eggs or cereal?"

Jason shut his eyes in great concentration.

"Dah dah dah dah dit dah."

"Okay Jason!" Kim said, patting him on the back. "I think you know about ten letters now."

"Eleven. A, e, i, o, s, t, h, m, n, j, and k. I can spell my name. Want to hear me?"

"You bet I do."

"Dit dah dah dah dit dah dit dit dit dah dah dah dah dit."

"My goodness, Jason, did Kim teach you that?"

His head bobbed up and down and Kim couldn't help grinning at Mrs. Gressner.

"We know the whole alphabet," Stacie and Julianna chimed in. "Want to hear us spell our names too?"

For awhile it looked like breakfast was going to be lost to code, but Kim and Mrs. Gressner managed to keep buttoning clothes and combing hair as the dits and dahs continued.

"I think that's incredible," Amy Gressner said to Kim as they walked to the dining hall.

"Well you know learning a foreign language is easiest when you're young — that's why kids in bilingual families pick up the language of both parents without really thinking about it. Morse Code is just another language and the kids like it because it's kind of secret. We can talk to each other and no one who doesn't know code can tell what we're saying."

"I'm not sure that's so good," laughed Grant Gressner.

"Did you ever hear the story of Samuel Morse's romance?"

Kim asked him.

"I don't think so. Was it an electrifying relationship?"

"Oh Grant," his wife protested.

Kim laughed at the two of them.

"Well maybe in a way it was. The woman he was in love with came from a very proper family so all courtship had to take place in the drawing room under the watchful eyes of her parents. So Samuel Morse taught her his code and the two of them sat there and quietly held hands while they secretly tapped love messages back and forth. It came as a great surprise when Samuel asked her father for his daughter's hand in marriage — as far as the parents knew, nothing had developed between them at all."

"Dit dit dit dit dit," the children's father said, kissing his wife on the cheek as they walked into the dining room.

****

On a lower deck, Orlando sat at a table by himself eating breakfast. On some cruises, performers were given fancy suites and dining room privileges. Orlando didn't quite rate that. He was getting sleeping quarters, a small salary, and food with the ship's staff.

Ferdy was his only contact on board, and Orlando was very careful that no one ever saw them together. And he made it clear he wasn't interested in making friends with the other staff. There was something about the dark magician that kept people at a distance anyway. Orlando didn't mind the solitude. He gazed out across the ocean and went over plans once again in his mind.

He thought the Gressner kid was going to work out. Definitely the right size — wouldn't want one any bigger. And he thought the boy liked him. In fact, he was darned well sure the boy idolized him. But there was always the unforeseen. If for some reason, the kid didn't come to the performance, then either of the two Green boys might work although his instinct told him the Gressners were worth more. The Greens looked like the kind who were more showy with their wealth — might not have a lot in the bank because the wife was wearing it all.

Well, he would just have to see what developed. He'd checked the syringe full of ketamine this morning. It was carefully wrapped in a towel in the bottom of his drawer.

He'd never actually seen the stuff work, but a buddy of his in the prison infirmary had told him it would.

He worried a little about Ferdy. The guy was scared - - but he was relying on his greater fear of being sent to prison to keep him going.

The land part of the operation worried him a bit more. Mitch was in charge of that. For half the take, he'd better do a good job too. There would be no cheating Mitch — they were equal partners in this. He had talked to him by phone the night before they sailed. Mitch said everything was in place. Not a problem in the world.

One of the ship's officers walked by and nodded to Orlando and he nodded back.

"No magic today? I understand you got pretty good reviews. I heard kids talking about you during the bridge tour."

"Thanks. No, I'm resting up my magical powers."

The officer laughed and walked on. Orlando got up and walked over to the rail. Passengers were starting to disembark. Most were still at breakfast — the major exodus would begin in about a half hour. He would wait until the crowd thinned and then wander ashore himself. He certainly didn't have any desire to sightsee. What would he do? Go on the boat tour to Alcatraz? He smiled at the idea.

No, he would just take a stroll up Fisherman's Wharf, get a beer or two, and then at noon, he'd make the phone call.

Chapter 7

San Francisco

Sunday, June 17th
San Francisco

S an Francisco was everything Kim anticipated and more. From the clanking cable cars to the colorful smells and sights of the wharf area to the hundreds of little shops crammed into China Town, she felt she couldn't take it all in.

With Jason's hand firmly clutched in one hand and Stacie's in the other, she followed Mr. and Mrs. Gressner with Julianna. The kids were real troopers for the first two hours, touring the city by taxi and on foot, but then they began to tire.

"Let's stop here and get a bite to eat," Amy Gressner suggested.

"Eat? We've got a whole floating restaurant sitting right there at the dock. Let's go back to the ship," her husband said in his grumbling indignant tone which Kim had quickly learned was his way of teasing his wife.

"Grant... it's a mile back to the ship. The kids need to eat something now."

"So we can build up our energy, Dad," Julianna said, hugging him.

"It's hopeless," he said turning to Kim with a smile.

"I'm totally outnumbered. No one seems to be fiscally responsible around here except me."

"Grant..."

"What's fizz — fizza something?" Stacie asked.

"Money!" her father told her, rumpling her curls. "It means not spending all your money."

"I didn't," she said solemnly, opening her small purse. "See — I still have four dollars of the money Grandma gave me."

"Atta girl — I'm going to hire you as my assistant plant manager."

Kim sat back in her chair, just enjoying the view down the street. The Gressners were such pleasant people. They all seemed to have a truly good time together. It was a beautiful day, lunch had been ordered, she was in nice company... and tomorrow she'd see Marc.

"What are you thinking about?" Julianna asked. "You look really happy."

"I am," Kim said. "I'm happy to be with you guys."

Jason, in particular, thought that was a great answer. He climbed out of his chair and into Kim's lap where he promptly went to sleep.

****

"Mitch?"

"Yeah, Leo, I'm here, just like I said I'd be."

Orlando looked behind him to make sure no one was waiting for the pay phone.

"You got a place?"

"Yeah — safe as can be."

"Where?"

"I'll show you tomorrow."

"Mitch, I'm trusting you on this one — everything had better be in order."

"It is — don't worry."

"Got the cell phones?"

"Yup — three of them sitting right in the van. Okay — now what time do you want me there?"

"Seven thirty-five. I plan to do it right at seven thirty two — should take me less than three minutes to get off the ship. You be there — you understand?"

"Yeah, yeah, Leo — just relax."

"Mitch?"

"Yeah?"

"What color is the van?"

"Black. I'll be in the loading zone just a little north of where the ship docks."

****

By the time the children had walked back to the ship, they truly were tired, and to Kim's surprise didn't offer any resistance to the idea of a nap. Their father said that was an excellent idea, that he would lie down for awhile too, and that Kim and Amy could go shopping.

Kim put a bandaid on a blister forming on her heel, changed her flats for tennis shoes, and declared that she was ready TO SHOP.

"Should I send a Brinks truck along with you two?" Grant Gressner asked smiling.

"No — way too obvious. The credit cards will do nicely, dear."

"That's what I was afraid of."

Kim and Amy Gressner walked down to the Main Deck where the gangplank connected them with the dock.

"How many miles do you think we've already walked today?" Kim asked.

"Probably about six. Well, at least this way, we can eat the Baked Alaska tonight at the Captain's Dinner and not have to worry."

"Now there's a thought," Kim laughed as she picked up her stride.

The two of them caught a taxi to the downtown shopping district and for the next three hours spent the time doing the stores. Kim bought a necktie with a bass guitar on it for Marc and a tourist-type t-shirt for herself. Amy Gressner found a few Christmas gift items, but even so the two were not heavily laden as they made their way back to the ship at 4 p.m.

The kids, of course, were wide awake and ready to play. "Swimming, Kim! Let's go swimming."

Actually, the idea of cool water sounded refreshing. Perhaps, the energy of the children was contagious, but after a half hour of romping with them in the Sun Deck pool, she did feel somewhat revived. They hurried back to the cabin to shower and change for the Captain's dinner.

****

"What are you doing here?"

Orlando looked up in surprise as Ferdy let himself into his cabin where Orlando was relaxing on the bunk.

"I just came to check on things. Are you still going through with this idea?"

"Of course I am. What do you mean am I going through with it?"

"Just seems like a really dangerous plan — that's all. We might all wind up in prison."

"Look Ferdy, I know you're all clean and innocent and that guy you killed was just an accident — right? Well I'm not. Just by disappearing into Orlando's identity, I've already violated parole. Yeah, you're right — we could go to prison. You could even if I don't do this. So just keep your mouth shut and do what you're supposed to and after Monday, you'll never see me again."

****

Kim caught a glimpse of herself in the blue silk dress as they made their way down the corridors to the Captain's reception. The children were less than enthusiastic about standing in line to shake hands with the Captain, but they did so dutifully and seemed to enjoy his attention once they were introduced. Julianna even managed to run her fingers through her curls before the photographer took a photo of the captain bending over to shake hands with her.

Then it was time for the Captain's dinner. Kim tried to take it all in — everyone all dressed up — they could be going to a state ball. Julianna and Stacie were adorable in matching pink lace dresses, and Jason had reluctantly consented to wearing a bow tie with his white shirt and dark slacks. But when they were seated, his true nature came out.

"How do I eat in this?" he said, trying to pull the material from his white sleeves out of the way of the gravy on his roast beef.

"Here," Kim said as she rolled up his sleeves.

"So how do you like it so far?" Melanie asked her. "I looked for you this morning, but you were already gone."

"Oh I know — we ate up on the deck. Everyone wanted to get an early start going ashore. How do I like it? It's great. More luxury than I ever dreamed possible. How about you?"

"I'm already wondering when I can do this again," Melanie laughed.

"I'm sorry we haven't been able to spend more time together. It's just the kids keep me really busy."

"Oh, I understand. You're going ashore in Astoria. That's where your friend Marc will be, right?"

"Yes, but not until after the magic show — I promised the kids I'd go to it with them."

"We're going too!" Jessica Reeves added. "Did you know the magician is going to make somebody disappear?"

"Yes, I believe we have heard that," Kim said, grinning at Jason, Julianna, and Stacie. "In fact, I think we've heard that about twenty times a day."

****

54

Monday, June 18th
At sea

As fun as San Francisco was, Kim decided that she liked being at sea best. With the sea breeze blowing in her face as she walked along the deck early in the morning, she didn't think anything could be more perfect. She paused along the railing and watched the Northern California coastline emerging from its shroud of ghostly morning fog. It was 6:30 a.m.

Time for people to be going to work, she thought as she pulled out her handheld radio and punched in a repeater frequency in the Eureka area. It was quiet. Maybe no one was around.

"This is KA7SJP aboard the Sea Mystic somewhere near the California-Oregon border calling CQ and standing by."

"KA7SJP from WA7BLF. Name's Sally."

"Good morning, Sally; my name's Kim. Are you in Eureka?"

"Just outside — on my way to work. I'm an EMT with the local fire department. Looks like kind of a foggy day."

"Be patient, Sally. It's absolutely gorgeous out here at sea. I imagine your fog will lift shortly."

"I hope so. So you're aboard a cruise ship? Are you having fun?"

"Wonderful fun — it's my first cruise and it's great."

"My husband who, by the way is WA7BLE, and our youngest son, KB7MPD, took the Alaska Inside Passage cruise last year. Really spectacular."

"We're Headed to Seattle. I can hardly wait. You all have seven calls. Where are you from?"

"Washington — we've just been down here a few years."

Just then, Kim saw the waiters heading toward the dining room.

"Sally, I'm going to have to sign. I'm sort of a nanny for a family on this cruise and it's time to get the kids up. Thanks for the QSO."

"My pleasure, Kim — you have a great time. WA7BLF is clear."

"KA7SJP clear."

That was the only hamming Kim got a chance to do during the day. The children were so hyper, particularly Jason, that she was practically at her wit's ends trying to keep them occupied. They dreamed up errands that took them past the Count's Lounge and every five minutes, Jason asked her how much longer until the magic show.

By the time dinner rolled around, he was practically ill with anticipation. He refused to eat a bite — just kept fidgeting in his seat. Kim had long since given up any idea that maybe the kids would just want to go ashore.

"You know if you'd like to go see Marc earlier, we can take the kids to the show," Amy Gressner said.

"Oh, it's okay. I promised them I'd go with them. And I can't really be with him until all the music performances are over."

The kids had looked anxious at the suggestion that Kim might not be going to Orlando's show, but at her reassuring words, they clung to her arms. Kim looked at Jason's still full plate sympathetically. Funny thing — she didn't seem hungry either.

****

Mitch Foler would have understood a quivery stomach. His own hamburger lay untouched on the seat beside him. That along with supplies he had discussed with Leo were all there as he drove back to his motel room to wait. Leo a.k.a. "Orlando" — Mitch still had to smile as he thought of his old prison buddy as a magician in a tuxedo — had told him to put some food supplies where they'd keep the kid. He wasn't going to argue with Leo, but he knew that the kid wasn't going to be able to eat.

Making a key for the lock had been easy. He could have just picked the lock each time, but they wanted quick and easy access. So he'd made a key, and last night about two in the morning, he had crept through the woods and put some juice and cereal there. The problem he hadn't thought about until then was that it was light until almost ten. What were they going to do with the kid until dark? Well, he'd think of something. He always did.

Chapter 8

"I Choose You"

Monday, June 18th
Astoria

Kim let the children drag her to the Count's Lounge at 6:45 even though it meant that they left dinner before dessert was served. The evening show was due to start at 7:00. Mr. and Mrs. Gressner stayed behind, promising to join them in time for the famous disappearing act.

Jason wasn't taking any chances on not being in the front row. He pulled away from Kim's grasp and ran to a prime seat. Julianna and Stacie settled in on either side of him. Kim sat with them until other kids began filing into the rows. Then, she moved to the back and put her sweater across the two seats next to her for the Gressners.

Orlando was five minutes late to the show, but when he entered, it was in the midst of swirling silver and red lights that glanced off his jet black hair, creating almost an underworld atmosphere.

"Ladies and Gentlemen, the Great Orlando!" Miss Lillan yelled at the top of her voice.

The room was packed now. Kim noticed the Reeves had come in too late to find seats. Like twenty others, they stood against the back wall. Just as she thought she might have to give up the saved seats, Amy and Grant Gressner hurried through the doorway and sat down beside her.

"Miss anything?" Mrs. Gressner asked.

"Any sawed off body parts or floating skulls from the last performance?"

"Oh Grant — just pretend you're a little kid again."

"Yes, dear, I will."

Kim smiled at him. His gentle teasing was obviously affectionate.

Orlando was doing something with spinning orbs which slowly lifted off the table, suspended as they shimmered in the lights.

"Probably monofilament fish line."

"Shhh, Grant — you're wrecking my concentration".

The audience was silent as Orlando closed his eyes, deep in concentration. Slowly, the three orbs joined into one and then settled to the table. The children were applauding even before he bowed.

He came to center stage and selected a little girl to assist with various ball and hoop tricks and then feathers that transformed into tiny American flags. He was really quite a bit better tonight than he had been Saturday, but even from her back row seat, Kim could see the sweat pouring off his face. She decided he must be building up his concentration for the disappearing act.

Finally, he patted the little girl on the head and sent her back to her seat. He brought a small blue box to the center stage and put a red ball in it.

"Want to see my Disappearing Act?" he asked.

"Yes!"

He opened the box and the ball was gone. There was silence in the room as kids turned to look at each other. Surely, this wasn't the disappearing act. Orlando laughed at their dismay.

"No, my friends, that's not the Disappearing Act I told you about. I just wanted to see if you were in the right mood. Everyone has to be in a very magical mood for this to work. Are you all in A MAGICAL MOOD?"

"YES!"

Not only did they shout their answer, but many clapped their hands as well. A few boys in the back added wolf whistles to the din.

"All right. Now I need a very special assistant. One who has magical powers him or herself."

A sea of waving hands blocked Kim's view. She wasn't sure if the Gressner children were among them, but she bet they were. Since Jason had already been a helper Saturday, perhaps one of the girls might be chosen tonight. Kim felt a chill run down her spine at the possibility of Julianna or Stacie standing up next to Orlando.

Just as he had in his previous performance, Orlando closed his eyes and waved his right arm back and forth acros the audience.

"I choose... I choose," he said.

"I choose you!" Orlando, said opening his eyes.

Kim let out a small gasp. He was pointing directly at Jason.

"I choose you!"

****

It was time to leave the motel. He didn't officially check out, but Mitch suspected that he wouldn't be coming back. Now that the actual time was approaching, it seemed like his whole plan was full of holes. Why hadn't Leo done this in San Francisco where there was more than one way in and out of town? And the whole underwater bit — it seemed pretty theatrical and downright stupid, now that he thought about it.

How long was this going to take, anyway? Leo said it would all be over in 24 hours. Well supposing it wasn't that easy.Supposing it took days, even a week? He felt sweat break out on his forehead as he loaded the last of his supplies into the back of the black van.

Despite the magic festival, there were still plenty of vacancies at this motel — five miles from town and kind of seedy, it wasn't exactly a tourist draw.

Accustomed to watching his back, Mitch glanced at the vacant motel office and climbed into the driver's seat. 7:15 p.m. He should arrive right on time.

****

Orlando repeated the words again in a commanding voice. His arm pointed unwaveringly at Jason. Julianna and Stacie shrieked with delight and grabbed their brother by the arms, urging him up on stage.

Jason sat paralyzed in his seat. He seemed so surprised that any reaction at all was beyond him. Several other children waved their hands in the air wildly, yelling.

"I'll go, I'll go — pick me!"

Orlando looked down at Jason and smiled. Jason turned his head slightly, and Kim could see that he was smiling back. Orlando walked down the stairs, came to the front row of children, and stopped in front of Jason. Everyone hushed to hear what the magician was saying.

"Saturday, when you helped me with the confetti box, I sensed a special magic quality in you. Would you like to be my assistant in the Disappearing Act?" Orlando said softly in an almost fatherly tone.

Jason looked up at him and nodded and then looked shyly back down at the ground. Orlando put out his hand and Jason took it. The two of them climbed back on stage.

Kim turned to see how Jason's parents were reacting to all this. His mother seemed a little concerned but when Jason smiled at Orlando, she smiled too. Orlando whispered something to Jason and he listened intently, nodding.

Orlando handed him a pair of scissors and then held a string taut between his hands. With just a little difficulty, Jason managed to cut the string in two. Orlando took the scissors and cut each string in two once more. Then he stuffed them all the pieces into a soup can and instructed Jason to put his hand in. Out came one intact string in his small hand. More applause. Jason and Orlando bowed together. Jason spotted his parents and gave a half wave.

"Where's the disappearing act?" Kim heard some kids ahead of her whisper.

As though he had heard their question, Orlando

paused dramatically and said, "And now for the disappearing act. My young assistant here — what's your name young man?"

Jason looked surprised at the question since Orlando had already called him by name in previous meetings, but he answered quietly.

"Jason... Jason Gressner."

"Well Jason Gressner — now that you've had a bit of on the job training, I want you to assist me with my most special trick. Are you ready?"

Jason nodded solemnly. Orlando handed him some black canisters to place at the edge of the stage. Orlando walked over and inspected each one carefully. Jason stood to his side. Orlando whispered something in his ear.

"Abracadabra," Jason said, waving his hand over one canister.

Orlando whispered in his ear again, and Jason, blushing, said it louder — "Abracadabra!"

This time a small wisp of mist began to float out of the can.

"C02," Mr. Gressner said to his wife and Kim.

Orlando and Jason repeated the procedure over five more black cans until a foggy haze began to drift out over the audience. There were nervous giggles from the front row as the chill of the vapors hit them. Jason and Orlando's feet became invisible as they moved through the growing clouds.

Some background music that had been playing softly now rose in volume. Jason and Orlando looked like silent movie characters as they scurried around the stage moving tables and chairs out of the way.

"So what's the big deal about that?" Mr. Gressner muttered. "He lets some carbon dioxide out of cans and we can't see their feet. Magic — hogwash!"

"Dear, don't be so cynical. I'm sure there's more to it than that," his wife reprimanded him.

Orlando unfurled a large red blanket which he gave to Jason to hold. He made sort of a ceremony out of opening the blanket, showing it to the audience, and then refolding it enough so that Jason could carry it.

His voice boomed through the growing fog as he and Jason descended the steps to the audience. Carrying the blanket, Jason obediently followed the magician up the aisle to the back of the room to the right of where Kim and Mr. and Mrs. Gressner sat. Jason grinned at his father. Mr. Gressner gave him the thumbs up signal.

Orlando whispered in Jason's ear and Jason carefully spread the red blanket out on the floor.

"Ladies and Gentlemen," Orlando's voice boomed. "I want you to watch this spot very carefully. This is the spot where my young assistant and I will reappear!"

Then extending his hand to Jason, Orlando ran with the young boy back up on stage. Now the audience was torn between watching the stage and focusing on the red blanket.

****

During a five minute break, Marc walked to the edge of the canopied area where he had a clear view of the dock. The Sea Mystic, lit up like a Christmas tree, was anchored in port, dwarfing the lighthouse ship, the Columbia.

He pulled his handheld from his pocket and gave Kim a quick call, but there was no answer.

Instead after a brief pause to make sure that Marc's call wasn't being answered by Kim, another voice came on the air.

"KA7ITR from KA7ITT — how's it going, Marc?"

"KA7ITT from KA7ITR — great Ann — how are you? I hope you're coming down for our jazz show tonight at nine."

"You bet — wouldn't miss it. Jerry's just finishing up in the greenhouses. We're going to grab a bite to eat here and then we'll be down."

Just then, the drummer signaled to Marc that they were starting up again. He signed with Ann and gave Kim another quick call. He didn't really expect her to answer as she'd told him she'd be in the magic show until eight. By then, he'd be in the thick of a performance following the mayor's proclamation of Magic Festival Week. He looked at his watch. Four and a half more hours until they could spend some time together.

It had only been a week since he had last seen Kim, and yet she was in his mind almost every waking moment — some of his sleeping ones too. Call it ESP or whatever, he sensed that she was thinking of him too. Could it be that Kim Stafford, straight A student, highly focused, "no time for a boyfriend," super competent ham radio operator was letting down her guard a little? That maybe she was having some of the same feelings he was?

Probably not, he told the gulls scavenging for crumbs on the sidewalk. I'm most likely imagining it. She'll get off the ship, say hi, and bye, and if I'm lucky in a month or so, I'll get to spend another five minutes with her.

A couple of the other musicians were making their way back inside. Marc gave a final glance at the berthed ship and hurried to catch up with them.

****

Ann Jensen whistled to "Patches." She tied a note that said "dinner" to her collar and then picked up a work glove that belonged to her husband, Jerry. The dog perked up her ears expectantly. To her, the games of hide and seek that her owner invented were wonderful fun.

"Here Patches."

Ann held out her husband's glove to the dog who sniffed it and wiggled with excitement.

"Seek!"

In a blur of black and white fur, the dog was off racing across the yard where Jerry was working in one of their five greenhouses that produced a steady supply of beautiful fuchsias for Oregon nurseries. Since his scent was everywhere, the dog would probably just find him by sight, but if by chance Jerry had walked out in the field beyond the last greenhouse, she knew Patches would quickly put her nose to the ground and track him.

Jerry was coming across the yard now, laughing as Patches circled him barking. Like Ann, he was a jazz enthusiast and was looking forward to hearing Marc perform tonight at the festival. Having him stay with them this week was almost like having their own kids at home.

****

Orlando dragged an even larger canister out to the front of the stage. Still holding Jason's right hand with his left, Orlando waved his right arm out over the audience for quiet.

"To make this work," he said almost shouting, "we all have to say 'Abracadabra' together. When I drop my hand, I want you to yell 'Abracadabra' as loud as you can three times — then count aloud to fifteen and then everyone — look at the red carpet."

Chapter 9

Disappearing Act

Monday, June 18th
Astoria

The music swelled to a crescendo. Children in the audience talked to each other excitedly as Orlando raised his right arm dramatically and then dropped it down, striking the lid off the red can.

The audience was well practiced with the magic phrase from the show Saturday night. With perfect clarity, they shouted "Abracadabra! Abracadabra! Abracadabra!"

Huge clouds of dark gray smoke billowed across the stage. Kim had one quick view of Jason's white scared-looking face and then the entire stage was obliterated.

****

Mitch Foler glanced at his wrist watch and moved his van into position alongside the dock. He was in a loading only zone, but if Orlando was on time, he didn't plan on being there long. And after all... they were loading.

****

Several children let out cries of alarm as the smoke drifted down from the stage, making them cough.

"I don't like this, Grant," Mrs. Gressner said to her husband.

"Remember to count!" someone yelled from the back row.

"One, two, three, four, five, six, seven, eight, nineteen, eleven, twelve, thirteen, FOURTEEN, FIFTEEN!" the crowd cried triumphantly.

Mitch jumped at the voice.

"I'm sorry sir, but you can't park here — it's a loading only zone."

He turned to see a uniformed security guard standing next to his driver's window.

"Oooh, I'm sorry. I was just waiting for my uh my wife — she's delivering something... uh... to our daughter who's working at the magic festival. She ought to be right back out."

"Well, I'm sorry, but you'll have to park in one of the lots or farther down on the street if you can find a place. There are all sorts of food deliveries being brought in here."

Mitch stared at the man who obviously wasn't going to move until he started the van and pulled out. Reluctantly, he turned the key and eased out of his prime spot in direct line of the ship's gangplank.

He felt himself perspiring as he drove down the street, looking for a place to turn around. Traffic was pretty heavy with all the comings and goings of the festival and it was a good three blocks before he found a place to hang a u turn and make his way back. He held his breath as he came back up to the loading zone area.

He cursed. An ice cream truck was parked in the yellow loading zone and two men were busy transferring huge cartons of ice cream onto a hand truck.

****

All heads turned toward the red blanket. Kim tried to peer through the smoke which was dissipating some, but it was impossible to see anything on stage.

The audience grew quiet again except for the children coughing in the front rows. Orlando's music continued at its deafening pitch.

"Where is he, Grant?" Mrs. Gressner said, her voice rising in fear.

"Probably running madly down the halls to get here through the back door — just relax, dear."

Kim glanced at her watch. Two minutes had gone by. She stared hard at the doorway right behind the red carpet, listening for the sound of footsteps.

****

Mitch didn't want to go into the Maritime Museum parking lot — too slow to get out. Besides, it looked full. Just as he was half a block beyond the loading zone, a car pulled out of a spot on the opposite side of the road. Mitch eased the van into it. The security guard who was walking the length of the sidewalk, spotted him and waved. Mitch waved back.

****

There were nervous titters of laughter as the smoke cleared, showing a very empty stage and an even emptier red carpet.

"Hoax!" someone yelled.

"Great trick — do it again," a teenage boy jeered from the back.

After a couple more minutes of restless waiting, Miss Lillan and another young woman from the cruise entertainment staff approached the stage hesitantly. This was definitely not the way Orlando had explained the act to them. Still, they hated to be up on stage looking for him when he burst in the back door.

****

Mitch looked at his watch. 7:35. Where was he?

****

Miss Lillan had dealt with performers' delicate temperaments before, and her first impression of Orlando was that he was not someone she wanted to anger. But there was no denying Mr. and Mrs. Gressner who were on their feet, hurrying toward the steps.

"Jason? Jason, where are you?" his mother called tentatively.

"Sue, check the hallway," Miss Lillan said to her assistant.

Sue, a trim raven-haired woman in the ship's blue and white outfit, hurried to the back door. Kim was already standing in the open doorway, peering down the empty hall.

"It's probably just part of the act," Sue told her.

"Well, I don't think it's very funny," Kim said. "Poor Jason is probably scared to death."

"Do something!" Amy Gressner implored her husband onstage. By now, several crew members, hearing the commotion, had come into the room and were searching backstage under boxes and behind curtains.

Mr. Gressner kicked a couple of the spent canisters aside and then bent over to pick up something from the floor.

"Oh no!"

He stood up holding an empty syringe in his hand. Miss Lillan took one look and hurried to a white phone on the wall.

****

Bingo! The ice cream truck delivery men slammed the back doors and climbed in the front. Mitch held his breath as they pulled away from the curb. Quickly, he started the van and made a u-turn.

A car ahead of him slowed as it came to the loading zone.

"Pull into it and I'll kill you," Mitch hissed in the quiet of his van.

The car continued down the street. Mitch pulled the van into the spot and waited. 7:38.

****

"What has happened to my little boy?" Mrs. Gressner sobbed. "Why would anyone... how could... oh I know I didn't like the looks of that fellow..."

Her sobs increased until her whole body was shaking convulsively. A steward lowered her into a chair.

"Where's the stage exit?" Mr. Gressner demanded. "We've got to stop him!"

Miss Lillan was talking urgently on the phone to someone as Mr. Gressner and two stewards raced down the backstairs that led to an internal crew stairway to the main deck.

Stacie and Julianna, not quite sure what happened, but crying because their mother was, allowed Kim to gather them into her arms.

"Where's Jason?" Julianna cried. "I want my brother back."

"Me too," echoed Stacie.

"Shhh, he'll be back. Everything's going to be okay."

Kim wished she believed the words she was whispering in the girls' ears. From the moment she had first set eyes on Orlando, some instinct had told her the man was evil. Oh why had she let the children anywhere near him! Rage boiled up in her as she thought of Jason in that man's hands.

It was obvious that Mrs. Gressner was in no shape

to watch the girls, so Kim resisted her own urge to run after the men looking for Jason.

"Don't you worry — we'll find him," she said as she hugged the children to her tightly. "That's a promise."

She instinctively reached for her radio and then remembered she had left it in the cabin because there was no pocket in her dress or room in her evening bag to carry it.

Should she run back and get it? She looked at the two small girls clinging to her for comfort and decided that she needed to stay where she was.

****

Timing is a magician's best friend, and for once in his life, it looked as though timing was perfect for Leo Kinelli. The smoke canister released its secretive cloak exactly as planned. Jason, standing right next to him holding his hand, barely reacted to the injection of quick acting Ketamine anesthetic he stabbed in the little boy's arm. His brief struggles were over in thirty seconds, and the gag Orlando slipped into his mouth muffled any cries.

The drug worked just as his friend in the prison infirmary had said it would. He had been nervous about the amount to give him — had guessed at his weight. Five minutes before the show started, Orlando peeked through the curtains and spotted Jason waiting in the front row. It was then that he'd decided for sure that he would be the target. In the privacy of a restroom, he'd loaded up the syringe and slipped it into his pocket.

It was fairly easy for the big man to stuff the forty pound unconscious child in his big black bag and hoist it over his shoulder. And easy to run down those steps to the gangplank.

"Good evening, Mr. Orlando," the security staff said as he walked rapidly down the wooden gangplank to the dock of Astoria. "Looks like you've got quite a bag of tricks there."

"Sure do," Orlando said cordially, trying hard not to appear out of breath. "And I'm due at the Magic Festival show in fifteen minutes so I'm going to have to hurry to set up."

"Want us to get someone to drive you? That bag looks heavy."

"No, I'm fine. It's just a block and I like to walk. Gives me a chance to go over my tricks mentally."

Before there was time for any more small talk, Orlando was on the dock, walking toward the main street of Astoria. No one noticed that he headed toward a black van south of the dock area rather than north toward the festival area.

"I love magic," one security guard told the other. "Sorry I couldn't have seen his show."

"Yeah, me too — never can understand how they make things disappear and reappear."

They had exactly two minutes to mull over their love of magic when the white security phone on the wall rang. As one of them answered it, the other turned to see three men pounding down the stairs. His necktie askew and his face flushed bright red, Mr. Gressner was the first to reach them.

"Orlando... " he gasped. "Did Orlando leave the ship?"

"Sure did, sir — just a couple of minutes ago — carrying a big bag of tricks."

"That was my son in the bag!"

For a minute, it looked like Grant Gressner might strike the guard, but the distraught father merely pushed him aside and bolted down the gangway.

"Wait, sir!"

One of the security guards chased after Mr. Gressner as the other turned to see a dozen crew members swarming down the stairs.

"We've got a kidnapping on our hands — secure this doorway. No one else leaves the ship. Captain is calling the Coast Guard and the Astoria police," one of the ship's officers said. "You... and you — go help them," he said waving two crew members after the running figures of Mr. Gressner and the steward.

Chapter 10

Where is Jason?

Monday June 18th, 8:45 p.m.
Astoria

The two men caught up with Mr. Gressner and the steward who were standing bewildered in the middle of Astoria's main street. Some tourists strolling by stopped as he frantically asked them if they'd seen a man in a black suit carrying a huge bag. They shook their heads no.

The four men ran down the street, darting into the few shops still open — desperately searching every alcove and recess. Nothing.

At the first intersection, Mr. Gressner stopped.

"You two go on down the main street. I'll try this one," he ordered.

"Wait sir. The Astoria Police are coming," a ship's officer told him.

This part of the street had been blocked off for the festival, but soon a local police car came past the "No Motorist" signs, slowly making its way through the crowd. Two middle aged uniformed men got out. Their name tags read Captain Gates and Sergeant Torrey.

"Find my son!" Mr. Gressner cried hysterically as he grabbed Captain Gates by the shoulder.

"Now just calm down, sir. What's going on here?"

Quickly, one of the crew explained the situation. Captain Gates' eyebrows raised with worry.

"Has the Coast Guard been called?"

"Yes sir — they're on their way."

"Okay, I'm going to get sheriff's deputies and the state police involved. We'll begin a search of the town, and the immediate coastline. Do we have any indication of a vehicle being involved?, " Captain Gates asked. "Hey, where are you going?"

Mr. Gressner broke loose from the group and ran down a side street yelling "Jason!" at the top of his lungs.

"Go with him," Captain Gates told Sergeant Torrey, "and when he runs out of steam, bring him back here. I need to question him."

****

The bag on the floor was beginning to move as Jason fought through the anesthetic toward consciousness. Mitch turned worried eyes toward Orlando as the boy groaned and writhed. Watching in his rearview mirror for any pursuers, he pushed the van toward its limit along Highway 30 heading north out of Astoria.

"Can you give him some more stuff to knock him out? There's going to be a little delay before we stash him."

"Delay?" Orlando roared. "Whadya mean delay?"

"The place I've got arranged is too visible to go to until dark."

Orlando's groan overshadowed Jason's. A mix of fury and desperation covered his face as he waited for an explanation from Mitch.

"Look, Leo — it's the perfect place — old abandoned army bunker at Fort Stevens. I used to play there as a kid. All that live there now are ghosts. Everything's set up and no one will find him, but it's just going to take a little time to get him in."

Just then, Jason's arm thrust out of the top of the bag. In a few swift movements, Orlando pulled back the top of the bag, gagged and bound the child and then stuffed him back into it.

"No, I'm not going to give him more stuff. He has to be awake enough to talk for that first phone call, so you'd better think of something fast."

Mitch pulled onto a dirt road that led deep into a stand of wind-bent Shore Pine.

"Whoa," Orlando cautioned. "There's another van down there."

Mitch kept driving. He turned a weathered face toward his prison buddy.

"Like I said, I've got everything arranged. On the remote chance that someone noticed this van while I was waiting for you or ... well you never know how clues are going to come together. Anyway, I just thought it would be better if we started with a fresh rig."

"Where'd you get it?"

"Stole it — but it was behind a fishing cabin and I happen to know the people who own the cabin only show up on weekends. I've kind of been watching them."

"Yeah, I bet you have. Surprised you haven't ripped them off before this."

"Leo! Remember, we reformed — no more jobs until the big one. And then we're retired for good. I was just kind of watching them to see what it was like to be rich enough that you could have an extra vehicle just for weekend recreation."

Jason let out small terrified whimpers through the gag. Mitch looked at Orlando.

"You know that's going to get old in a hurry."

"That's why I want to dump him so we don't have to listen to it," Orlando said. Sweat ran down his face as he spoke.

****

Mr. Gressner ran down the dark alleys until the ache in his lungs overtook the ache in his heart. Bending over, his hands on his knees, he stood gasping while Sergeant Torrey caught up to him.

"Sir," the police officer said gently. "Why don't you

come on back with me? The captain wants to ask you some questions."

"But we've got to find him," Mr. Gressner said between gulps of air.

"Yes, sir, we've got people beginning to search right now. Maybe if we talk to you, we can come up with some clues that may help."

Mr. Gressner just shook his head back and forth, but he allowed the sergeant to take his arm and lead him back down the street to where Captain Gates was waiting. A small group of searchers — sheriff's deputies and volunteers — and a few ham radio operators (due to Kim's managing to get to her radio shortly after the incident) — gathered around Captain Gates as he gave instructions.

Working in pairs so that at least one armed deputy was with each volunteer, they dispersed in all directions, shining flashlights against the increasing darkness to search for Orlando and his captive.

"Why would anyone want to take our little boy?"

"That's what we aim to find out, sir," said Captain Gates, gesturing for Jason's father to sit down beside him on the wrought iron bench in front of the Astoria Ice Cream Parlor.

Jason's father sank down on the bench.

"All you're looking at are the doorways. He could be in any one of these buildings."

"I assure you, sir, that we're going to search every square inch of this town. I've ordered roadblocks on the main highways to check all cars going in and out."

Grant Gressner looked at the captain and then buried his face in his hands.

"We need your help to figure this out. I know you're under a huge amount of stress, but I want you to try and answer some questions."

"Okay," Jason's father said quietly.

"First of all — have you ever seen this magician guy before?"

"Not before the cruise, but we did several times on the ship since we left Ensenada. And I think he talked to each of the children. They all seemed excited about going to his magic show."

"I need your full name and the names of all those traveling with you."

"Gressner, Grant Gressner. My wife is Amy Gressner. Then there's Julianna's who's eight, Stacie, who's six, and Jason who's four. Almost five," he added wiping tears from his eyes.

Mr. Gressner's voice caught in a half sob, but he cleared his throat and continued.

"And Kim Stafford, our babysitter. She's nineteen and traveling with us."

"Do you know if Kim talked to this man?"

"Well yes, I think she did — she said something about his sitting down in the cafe with her."

"I'll want to talk to her, then."

"Okay — she's back on the ship with Amy and the girls. Ohhh poor Amy — I bet she's hysterical. I'd better get back to her."

"In a minute, sir. We'll both go back together. Now, some very important questions. Do you have any idea why anyone would want to take your child?"

"None, whatsoever."

"What do you do for a living?"

"I'm the owner of Computrex. It's a firm that makes computer software, especially games."

"How much money do you make, sir?"

"What's that got to do with?... oh, I see what you're thinking. Ransom, right?"

"Right. Do you make enough to be a target?"

Again, Grant Gressner buried his face in his hands.

"Yes, yes I do — a big target. But how would that guy know that? I've never seen him before."

"That's what we've got to try and figure out. Is your name in the papers much?"

"Yes, all the time in the L.A. area, and my wife's too. She's involved with all sorts of charity. There was a big article about me just two weeks ago in the business section of the L.A. Times. Outlined the phenomenal growth of our company."

Mr. Gressner rubbed his hand back and forth across his forehead.

"I think we should go back to the ship now and talk to the others. The Coast Guard will be there. Are you okay, sir?"

Mr. Gressner stood up and appeared for a moment like his knees might buckle under him.

"Yeah, let's go," he said, climbing into the police car.

Captain Gates got in and the two sped off toward the Sea Mystic pulled up to the dock. Within minutes, they were climbing the gangway. The security guards looked at Mr. Gressner sympathetically as they stood back to let him pass.

"Sir, the Coast Guard officials are on the bridge with the ship's captain."

"Tell them, I'll be right there. Where is Mr. Gressner's family?"

"Back in their cabin — Miss Lillan is with them."

In a daze, Grant Gressner led the police officers to their two cabins on the Regalia deck. The doors were standing open, and he paused for a moment before going in.

His wife's tear-stained face looked up at him hopefully, but one glance told her that Jason had not been found. Miss Lillan sat on the edge of the bed with her, holding her hand.

Kim came to the doorway joining the two rooms, both of the little girls standing by her side.

"Did you find him?" Julianna asked.

Mr. Gressner shook his head and Kim turned the girls back to their cabin. She knew the last thing Jason's parents needed now was the girls' eager questions. She held her finger up to her lips for them to be silent, and the three of them sat down on one of the lower bunks and leaned up against the wall.

Captain Gates excused himself to go meet with the Coast Guard and the ship's captain.

Kim listened to Mrs. Gressner's muffled sobs through the wall. Hearing her mother cry, Stacie started to cry. Kim gathered her close.

"Shhh — Stace. We can't help anyone if we just sit and cry. Maybe if we think real hard, we can come up with a clue that will help find Jason."

"Why did Mr. Orlando take him?" Stacie asked tearfully.

"Because we have a lot of money," Julianna told her.

"We do?" Stacie said, her eyes big.

"Yeah, I heard Miss Lillan ask Mom if anyone would try to kidnap Jason for ransom."

"What's ransom?"

Kim held her finger up to her lips again for silence. Mr. Gressner was telling his wife about the chase through the streets.

"How could he just disappear?"

"I don't know. Captain Gates said he could be anywhere. He thinks he's being held for ransom."

"Oh Grant! Why would anyone do that to our little boy?"

"Mr and Mrs. Gressner?

Kim heard a new voice and peeked around the corner to see a man in a Coast Guard uniform standing in the doorway.

"I'm Lieutenant Nepsen from the Astoria Coast Guard. I just wanted to bring you up to date on what we're doing so far."

"Do!" Mrs. Gressner cried. "You need to find our son .That's what you need to do!"

"M'am we've secured the harbor. No boats will leave

or enter without being inspected by us. And we'll be assisting the ship's crew in questioning personnel on board."

"You really think they'd take him away by boat?"

"We're just trying to cover every possibility."

Mrs. Gressner broke into fresh tears and her husband put his arm around her.

Chapter 11

Orlando a.k.a. Leo Kinelli

Monday June 18th, 10 p.m.
Astoria

The sound of sirens interrupted the jazz concert in progress in front of an enthusiastic audience of several hundred. Annoyed at the high pitched sirens, Marc and the others tried to keep playing, but when everyone turned to look at the police cars gathering in the street, they put down their instruments.

All Marc could see were people gathered around two men — lots of arm waving and hysteria. He watched as several uniformed officers entered the pavilion area and started filtering through the crowd.

"What's going on?" he whispered to the drummer.

"Beats me — looks like they're looking for someone."

Marc pulled his tiny two meter rig from his pocket. Perhaps, Kim was watching from an upper deck and would have a better view of what was going on.

He called her but there was no answer. He left the transceiver on, turned the volume up, and slipped it in his shirt pocket. Now the audience was buzzing with speculation. A police officer came to the stage microphone, and the crowd quieted.

"Ladies and Gentlemen, we'd appreciate it if you'd all just remain seated. We have a situation in progress and for your safety and our investigation, we're requesting your cooperation."

"KA7ITR from KA7SJP."

Marc pulled the radio from his pocket.

"KA7ITR here — go ahead, Kim."

To his amazement, she broke into tears and seemed unable to talk. He felt his gut wrench. Kim who had remained calm through forest fires, bank robbers, and drug dealers — Kim crying?"

"Kim — what's going on?"

"Oh, Marc , a performer from the ship kidnapped Jason. Just took him from the ship. He's gone — everyone's looking for him."

****

"Grant, we need to get off the ship and help them look."

"Nobody's being allowed off. Haven't you heard the loudspeakers?"

Mrs. Gressner was silent. The repeated message that Kim had been hearing in the background was now clear.

"We regret the inconvenience, but all shore activities are being cancelled for the evening due to an investigation in progress. A list of on-ship activities is being posted in the Main Lounge."

"You mean we can't even go ashore to help?" Mrs. Gressner asked.

"M'am, we'll let you do whatever you want to do," Lieutenant Nepsen told her. "but the ship's captain, Captain Dirilica and I feel that the kidnapper may try to contact you. It's best to be where he thinks you are."

Kim didn't hear any more of the conversation because just then a steward appeared in the doorway.

"Kim Stafford? Captain Dirilica and Captain Gates would like to talk to you on the Bridge."

Miss Lillan came in and sat down with the girls as Kim got up to follow the steward.

The steward was silent as he walked ahead of Kim down the carpeted hallway. As they passed through the Main Lounge, she heard groups of people talking.

"What's going on?"

"Someone got murdered!"

"No, kidnapped, I heard."

"And they think the criminal's still on the ship."

"Oh my, just like the Orient Express — how dreadful!"

The steward opened a heavy gray door that said 'Crew Only,'and Kim followed him up a metal staircase. Captain Dirilica met them at the head of the stairs and ushered Kim into a small office next to the Bridge.

Captain Gates introduced himself and the three of them sat down in the leather chairs. Captain Gates had a pad of paper ready to take notes as he turned to Kim. She felt her heart pounding as she struggled to answer his questions.

"I guess I don't need to tell you what's going on," Captain Gates said. "I was down in the street when ham radio operators showed up to help search. I understand you sent them?"

"I hope that's okay," Kim said, blushing.

"Certainly — at this point we can use all the help we can get, and I know those folks who volunteered — all good people. Now let's see if you can help us some more."

Kim listened intently as the three of them questioned her.

Yes, she had talked to Orlando at breakfast that morning. Yes, he had asked in kind of a vague way about the children — but nothing specific. No, he hadn't asked anything about who their father was.

"Was there anything unusual you remember?"

"He made me feel kind of creepy."

"Creepy? How?"

"Oh, I don't know. He's got really ugly teeth and he kept smiling at me like he wanted to be good friends or something. I just had this feeling I wanted to get away from him."

"Did you mention that feeling to the children's parents?"

"No, the kids seemed to like Orlando, and they were looking forward to his magic show. I thought I was just being too critical. My dad says that's one of my faults."

To her embarrassment, she began to cry. The emotions of the past few hours — fear, anger, sadness, and now guilt that maybe she could have done something to prevent the kidnapping —overwhelmed her. Captain Dirilica looked at her with raised eyebrows.

"You are not to blame, young lady. I want you to go back to your cabin now, but if you think of anything at all that might help, come tell me immediately."

Kim had regained her composure.

"Listen," she said, pulling her radio out of her pocket.

"As you already know, I'm a ham radio operator and so is a friend of mine at the concert in town. I don't know how many there are in Astoria, but I'm sure they'll want to organize a net to help you whether it's with communications or actual searching. If you'll let me off the ship, I'd like to be part of that."

Captain Gates spoke.

"Oh — yes, I just received a message that a young man at the festival area was already coordinating Amateur Radio operators to help the volunteers searching. Is that your friend?"

"Marc? Yes."

"Kim, for right now — we'd appreciate it if you'd stay on the ship. I think you can be the most help to us right here — we may need more information from you as the evening goes on."

"So what happens tomorrow afternoon if he hasn't been found?"

"The ship will probably sail. The Gressners will have to make decisions as we go along, but let's just take it one hour at a time," Captain Dirilica told her.

He and Captain Gates stood up, indicating the interview was over. A steward appeared in the doorway.

"Miguel will escort you back."

Kim held her radio to her ear as she followed the tall steward down the metal stairs. She felt a small surge of hope as various hams checked in with their calls, offering themselves and vehicles for the search. With many eyes and ears, maybe Jason could be saved. She had no information to add, so she decided to stay off the air for the time being.

To Kim's surprise, the girls had fallen asleep. Miss Lillan was covering them up with the ship's blue and white blankets when she walked in. Stacie opened her eyes sleepily.

"Did you find him?"

"Not yet, Stace — go back to sleep."

A short gray-haired man in a navy blue suit sat in the other room talking quietly to Mr. and Mrs. Gressner. Mrs. Gressner saw Kim in the doorway and motioned for her to sit down with them.

"This is Mr. Baller, Kim. He's in charge of the entertainers. He's showing us Mr. Orlando's personnel file to see if there's mention of anyone we know."

Mr. Gressner picked up a piece of paper from the folder and held it to the light.

"It's a real signature all right," he said running his finger over the name at the bottom: "Joseph Milan, Cruise Director for Astro Cruise Lines."

"Oh yes," Mr. Baller told them. "He came with good recommendations even though he'd only been with Astro one season. The only reason they let him go was because they had a full line of entertainers booked centering around a jazz theme."

"We did our usual thorough security check on Orlando. He came in for a couple of interviews. Everything checked out."

Kim reached over and touched the file.

"May I?" she asked.

"Certainly."

She scanned the physical information — six feet, one hundred eighty pounds, black hair. It all seemed to match.

"Did you ask about his teeth?"

"What?"

"Orlando's teeth were discolored and crooked," Kim said. "That was my first impression of him — that he needed to go to the dentist."

Mr. Baller reached for the phone on the dressing table. He spoke to the ship's operator and then punched in a series of numbers. Kim and the Gressners watched.

"Joe? — this is Mike Baller over at Magical Seas. We've had a problem with the magician Orlando you recommended — in fact, a very big problem. He's apparently kidnapped one of our passengers."

"Yeah, I'm sure. He and the kid disappeared a couple of hours ago. We've got a full scale search going on in Astoria right now. I have a funny feeling about this guy though — just to make sure we're talking about the same guy, describe Orlando to me."

"Dark hair, right. Mustache, right. Pretty slender, right. How about his teeth?"

The furrow on Mr. Baller's brow deepened as he listened to the answer. He said good-bye and let out a deep sigh as he turned to the Gressners.

"Straight and white as an orthodontist's ad," he said.

Mr. Gressner stood up and began pacing the length of the small cabin.

"Who is this guy?"

"That's what we've got to find out," Mr. Baller told him gently. "I believe the police are dusting his room for fingerprints right now."

"I want to go back ashore," Mr. Gressner said, standing up.

"Sir, the searchers are doing everything possible. I think your wife needs you."

Grant Gressner looked at Amy's tear-stained face and put his arm around her.

"Besides, if what we think is happening here is correct, the kidnapper is going to contact you pretty soon about a ransom."

"I'll wring his neck," Gressner said, clenching his fists.

Amy Gressner began crying again. Kim got her a cold wash cloth from the bathroom.

****

He was so scared. Jason tried to thrash his way out of the dark bag, but the man in the van seat was holding the top shut. And that man was Orlando! Oooh — his brain felt fuzzy — kind of like when he woke up after a nap — and his tummy hurt.

His mind was a jumble of thoughts — standing on stage with Mr. Orlando and then that cold misty fog covering them both up. Something really bad had happened then. Someone had stuck something in his arm and then he was upside down. He could kind of remember the feel of rough fabric being pulled over his head.

Where was he? He wanted his mommie and daddy. Breathing hard like a captured wild animal, he shivered in the bag, hearing his own heart pounding in his ears. He kicked his feet as hard as he could but the bag held his legs bent behind him.

****

Somehow the night passed. Stacie and Julianna slept fitfully. Every time they woke up, Kim went in to comfort them. In between, she stood out on the small balcony attached to Mr. and Mrs. Gressner's room. She kept Marc up to date on what was going on aboard ship. He was working with another ham, driving the surrounding areas, looking for Orlando and Jason.

Somewhere around 2 a.m., she lay down beside Stacie and dozed for an hour. The sound of Captain Gates' voice in the next cabin woke her. She got up quietly and went to the doorway.

"We haven't had any luck with prints from his cabin — just too many on the doorknobs to make anything positive. And it looks like he was careful not to touch anything else in the place."

"The gas canisters and the syringe!" Kim suggested.

Captain Gates smiled at her.

"Young lady — thank you!"

He turned and ran down the hallway. The Gressners resumed their all night vigil, waiting for a phone call — waiting for any news about Jason. Two hours later, Captain Gates was back.

"You were right," he said to Kim. "We got a readable print off of the biggest canister. The computer came up with a match a few minutes ago. Orlando is really Leo Kinelli — just got out of prison six months ago. Several counts of armed robbery. We're checking on his records at the prison now."

Mr. Gressner nodded numbly and got up to stare out the window into the darkness.

"Our poor little boy," Mrs. Gressner cried softly.

Kim turned back to the cabin and lay down on her own bunk. So where would a kidnapper hide a little boy? Was he still in Astoria? She longed to be out looking for him herself. Jason's innocent face danced in her mind. She just had to do something to find him!

Chapter 12

Ransom Calls

Tuesday, June 19th
Astoria

I t was 2 a.m. before Orlando and Mitch felt secure enough to drive down the quiet road that led out to Fort Stevens. The once active Army facility had been reduced to a historical site decades ago. Although tourists still visited the small museum and walked through the main bunker system, the old WWII communications bunker, well hidden in the trees, was not utilized by anyone. Mitch said it was the perfect place to stash a kid.

Orlando wasn't so sure.

"There's only one way in and out," he complained as Mitch drove the van along the dark road.

"Yeah, but it's far enough from Astoria that people aren't going to be searching here."

"We have to go back and forth though, and we already saw that one roadblock on the coast highway."

"Don't worry. This is the only trip we have to make here, and I know some back roads back down to Seaside. We'll just drop him in here and that will be that."

Orlando looked over at Mitch. This was something he hadn't figured on. He had planned that if the Gressners coughed up the money, they'd get their kid back — he had no real desire to kill him. It was obvious Mitch didn't care — in fact, it kind of sounded like he expected the kid to die.

"Is this bunker underground?"

"What do you think bunker means, Leo?"

"Okay — well we need to make a phone call then before we put him in. I don't think the cell phone will transmit from underground."

Orlando looked down at the still bag at his feet. Around midnight, Jason had given up his struggling and whimpering. Whether it was from fright or exhaustion, the boy was either unconscious or asleep. They'd have to wake him up.

****

It's hard to know what goes on in the mind of a four ("almost five") year old child. Jason had verbal skills beyond his age — he knew his alphabet, could almost read, and as Kim could attest, was learning the code lickety-split.

In any other situation, he probably could have behaved in almost adult fashion. But the sheer terror of his abduction was beyond his coping skills.

He struggled at first and then his brain initiated a survival technique of simply withdrawing from the situation. He quit fighting and drifted into a near coma-like sleep. When Orlando pulled him out of the bag, at first he just stared at his captors.

Orlando put his face close to the that of the small boy.

"Listen, kid, your daddy wants to talk to you. See this phone here — you can talk to him. Maybe he'll come get you."

****

The phone ringing in the Gressner cabin jolted Jason's parents. Captain Gates cautioned Mr. Gressner as he reached out to grab the phone.

"Whatever he says, just agree with him — and try to keep him on the line as long as you can. We've got a trace on it."

"Hello? ... Jason? Oh don't cry, honey. Are you okay?"

In the doorway, Kim felt hot tears spring to her eyes at the sight of Mrs. Gressner's anguished face. Apparently, Jason was only allowed to speak briefly. Mr. Gressner steeled his face as he answered Orlando.

"Where is my son? Why have you done this?"

He was quiet for a minute, listening intently.

"Yes, yes, I understand — but that's a lot of money. When do you want it? That's absolutely impossible."

Whatever the kidnapper was saying, it was angering Grant Gressner. His face grew dark with frustration.

"Let me talk to Jason again. Hello?"

Sighing, Mr. Gressner placed the phone back and turned to Captain Gates.

"He hung up. Three million dollars if we want to see our son alive again."

Amy Gressner gasped.

"Says he'll call back later to tell us where and when he'll pick it up."

Speaking in shuddering breaths, Amy Gressner asked about Jason.

"What did he say — do you think he was okay?"

The boy's father seemed overcome.

"He just said...just said 'Daddy — Daddy I'm cold.'"

It was too much for Kim. She excused herself and went out on the deck. 3:00 a.m. She pulled out her radio and called Marc. No answer but another voice came back to her.

"KA7SJP from AA7RW. Kim, this is Lynn. Marc's sleeping for an hour. We're taking shifts. Any news?"

"Yes, the kidnapper just phoned and demanded ransom. Jason's alive. But we don't know any more than that. Apparently, he's going to call back."

"No clues as to location?"

"Not yet. I think they tried to run a trace on the call. I'm going to go back inside in a minute and I'll find out."

"Okay Kim, keep us informed. We've got about

twenty hams helping so far. Right now, they're working with the sheriff's department on searching and road check points."

"I wish I were there helping too, Lynn. The police captain asked me to stay here overnight though."

"Until we get more information like if the guy was in a car or something, there's not much we can do. Let me know if they can tell if the call came from Astoria."

"I will. I'm sure you'll all know as soon as we do. Captain Gates is with the Gressners now."

"Kim, why don't you get some sleep — we're taking turns out here."

"I'll see, Lynn — right now, I feel pretty awake."

****

She did manage to fall asleep for an hour, but at dawn, Kim woke and tiptoed to the doorway. Jason's parents were fast asleep in the chairs by the sliding glass door of their cabin. Kim looked at their hands still intertwined, sorrow visible on their tired faces even in sleep.

After brushing her teeth and washing her face, Kim smoothed her rumpled clothes and slipped on a jacket. Mrs. Gressner stirred in her sleep and mumbled something. Quietly, Kim let herself out into the hall and climbed the stairs to the outdoor cafe on the Promenade deck.

The sun was rising, a beautiful golden ball over the blue-gray Pacific Ocean. A few people strolled the decks as if nothing in the world were wrong — as if Jason Gressner were still asleep in his bunk like a four year old child should be. Kim shivered from fatigue and the early morning chill. Ferdy, their dining room waiter, was helping to set up the outdoor buffet. At the sight of Kim, his face flushed, and he turned and disappeared into the kitchen.

Odd, Kim thought, but she had more on her mind than the social graces of waiters. Quickly, she loaded up a tray with three cups of steaming coffee and some rolls and turned to take it back to the cabin.

Off the starboard side of the ship, she could see that the entire town of Astoria appeared to be asleep. Not a soul on the dock leading toward the main street. Somehow, Kim expected to see lines of police cars. Nothing. Just a quiet coastal town waiting to wake up.

****

Behind the scenes, Astoria was anything but quiet. During the night, F.B.I. officers had driven over from Portland. A temporary command center had been set up at the local police station. Including the twenty ham radio operators, about fifty volunteers were now organized into search teams. Problem was — no one really knew where to search. It was always possible that Orlando had driven directly to Portland or north into Washington.

The call came seven hours after the abduction — he could have gone a long way. But would he? If he planned on collecting ransom money in Astoria, would he leave the area? They didn't know that yet — wouldn't know that until he made his second call.

A trace on the phone had revealed that the number was a cellular phone belonging to Josh Harris, an orthopedic surgeon at a Portland hospital. The police contacted him and he insisted that yes that was his number, but that his phone was right beside him. Could someone be using his number without his knowledge? Yes, they could, the police told him.

"So that's his game," Captain Gates said. "Well we'll stop that line. The phone company is arranging a new number with Dr. Harris right now."

"But how will the kidnapper call us if his number won't work? Ooh, I don't think you should do that." Amy Gressner said.

"Listen, Mrs. Gressner. He wants to talk to you even more than you want to talk to him. If he doesn't tell you where to put the money, he's not going to get it. So if his phone doesn't work, hopefully, we'll force him to use a conventional one and maybe we can get a location on him."

****

Orlando raised up one elbow and looked at the sixty year old man snoring beside him. From Fort Stevens, they had driven south to Seaside, skirting Astoria entirely. Well at least Mitch had thought some things out. He had a motel room and the two of them slipped in unnoticed.

Within five minutes, Mitch was asleep. Orlando lay awake and wondered if the ransom plan would work. Three hours until he would phone again. And would they get back to the kid? Deep in his brain he knew the answer to that. They wouldn't.

As per his request, Mitch had placed some juice and cereal down in the bunker. Orlando looked at it when they dropped the kid off, but unless they ungagged him, there was no way of feeding him. And if they ungagged him, he'd yell. It seemed kind of stupid leaving the food right there beside him all tied up, but that's what they did.

****

Where was he? Jason's eyes opened wide in the darkness. It had taken him over an hour to be brave enough to open them — he was afraid if he did, he would see those two men again — the ones who dragged him in this dark cold place and tied him up. Tied his hands and feet so tightly that they hurt and then became numb.

He thought one of them was Orlando, the magician, but how could that be? Orlando had been a nice man. This man was terrible. He never once talked to him except when he took the gag out of his mouth and thrust the phone to his mouth. Ohhh — for a just few seconds he had heard his daddy — his strong daddy who could come and find him and take him away from this place.

Then they had put the gag back in his mouth and carried him down some steps and dropped him on the ground. There were sounds down here — scurrying sounds — and the steady rapid thumping of his own heart. He was so cold and so scared and so thirsty... and he wanted his mommy and daddy.

****

Amy Gressner's hands were shaking, trying to hold a cup of coffee which Kim had just brought her. It had only been minutes since Orlando's second phone call. He had made his demands quickly.

Three million in a waterproof bag to be hung from a buoy in line with the old deserted cannery north of town. The money should be placed there at 9 p.m. tonight. After he had made sure it was all there, he would phone them at 10 p.m. There was a pay phone on the dock where the ship landed. He had the number. They were to make sure they were there at ten... if they wanted to know where their kid was.

"I don't know if I can get the money that fast!" Mr. Gressner had protested. "You've got to give me some time."

Apparently, Orlando was unsympathetic to time constraints because Mr. Gressner rubbed his forehead, his eyes frantic.

"Jason — let me talk to Jason!" he pleaded. The cabin was silent as Grant Gressner held the phone in his hand, the dial tone audible for everyone to hear.

"Three million by nine tonight." "Oh Grant — three million? How can we get that?"

"Now wait a minute, folks," Captain Gates interjected.

"Don't tell me what to do!" Mr. Gressner snapped. "We're going to do exactly what this jerk wants — we ARE going to get our little boy back — do you understand?"

He took one look at the police captain's concerned face and then apologized.

"I'm sorry — forgive me. It's just that this is... this is unbearable."

The captain put his hand on Mr. Gressner's shoulder.

"I understand sir — now let's approach this one step at a time."

****

Within five minutes, the phone rang again. A trace had been made to a Portland number owned by Mr. and Mrs. David Jenks. A squad car was being sent to their house. It took less than thirty minutes for a supervising officer to call again with the results of that visit.

David and Sylvia Jenks were co-owners of a retirement home. They, themselves, were in their sixties. Yes, they owned a cellular phone — they showed it to the officer. Yes, that was their number on the traced call. But they could assure the nice officer that their phone had not been out of the house. Was there any way someone could use their number without their knowing? Yes, there was indeed, the Portland Police officer told them.

"So he's got more than one cellular number on him — maybe several. Okay," Captain Gates said calmly, "we'll just proceed with the next step."

The Gressners didn't ask what that step was because it seemed pretty obvious at this point that nobody knew.

****

By 10:00 a.m., law enforcement personnel including F.B.I. agents had completed their questioning of every person they could find who had been in the vicinity of the dock at the time of Orlando's escape. The only person who had a possible clue at all was a museum security guard who had been walking on the sidewalk.

He hadn't seen Orlando, but fifteen minutes before the time of the kidnapping, he'd had to ask a gray-haired man in a dark van to move out of the loading zone. The man had said he was waiting for his wife. Reluctantly, he'd left, but later just as the guard was going back into the museum to use the restroom, he'd noticed the van was back. If it was still there when he came back, he said he would have asked him again — this time not so nicely — to leave. But the van was gone when he came back out.

Did he have the license number? Sure. That was routine. Anytime he noticed a parking violation, he automatically wrote down the license. Just let him get his notepad back at the office.

Chapter 13

Request for Funds

At 10:30 a.m. Tuesday, the distraught Gressner family disembarked from the Sea Mystic. The ship wouldn't be leaving until later that afternoon, but the Gressners had opted to get a motel room so they could be closer to the police station and the ongoing search.

Melanie Reeves hugged Kim.

"I wish I could come with you and help, Kim."

"Thanks, Melanie, I wish you could too, but I don't think there's much that isn't being done already." Melanie tapped her handheld transceiver.

"Will you stay in touch until we leave?"

"Yes, I promise."

The two girls said good-bye tearfully. Captain Dirilica escorted the family down the gangplank and kissed Mrs. Gressner on the cheek.

"My dear lady, be brave. Our company will assist the police in every way to recover your son."

Mrs. Gressner nodded sadly. It was no use pointing blame now, but in her heart she wondered how anyone could have hired an evil man like Orlando. Her husband shook the ship captain's hand, and then Captain Gates led them, along with Julianna and Stacie, toward his police car to drive to a nearby motel.

"We have a lot of work to do in the next twelve hours. In fact I've cleared a couple of extra rooms for my men and some more F.B.I. agents who should be arriving soon."

"Kim!"

Kim turned to see Marc running down the sidewalk toward them. She'd been too busy taking care of the girls to try to contact him on the radio.

He gave Kim a quick hug but then turned to the Gressners and Captain Gates.

"I'm Marc Lawrence," he said extending his hand, first to Mr. Gressner. He shook hands with each of them solemnly including Stacie and Julianna who looked at him with awe.

"Captain Gates — do you know Ann and Jerry Jensen here in town?"

"Fuchsias, right?"

"Yeah, right. Did you know they have a dog trained to track? It's been used for search and rescue in disasters."

"I believe someone's bringing a tracking dog from Portland — should be here by noon."

"This one's available right now, and I understand she's pretty good."

"Bring her on down. The problem though is we have to have a trail to follow and the little boy was carried. We could try tracking the magician."

Captain Gates turned to another officer.

"Would you drive Mrs. Gressner and her daughters to the motel. I'm going to go back on board and see if we can get an item of Orlando's clothing."

****

Not only did Captain Gates come back with the sheets from Orlando's bunk, but before Mrs. Gressner left for the motel, she opened one of their bags and gave him a T-shirt that Jason had worn the day before. The police captain handled the items gingerly with protective gloves and dropped them into separate plastic bags so that their scents wouldn't be mingled.

Kim hugged the girls good-bye before they left. Amy Gressner's parents were on a plane right now heading to Portland from San Diego. They should arrive about one and they would drive to Astoria and take the girls back home with them until this terrible mess was over.

"Listen Stacie and Julianna," Kim said as they climbed into the police car. "I have to help her a little while, so if I don't get back to the motel before your grandparents come, I'll talk to you later on the phone. You two be good --okay?"

"Are you going to help find Jason with your radio?"

"I'm sure going to try."

She waved good-bye to them and then joined Marc while Mr. Gressner talked to Captain Gates. Marc was starting to walk toward the dock and she ran to join him. Kim slipped her hand into his.

"You know," he said looking at her with feeling, "if this weren't so horrible, our relationship would almost seem comical. Do you realize the only time we seem to get together is when something awful happens?"

"I know," Kim said, shaking her head. "Sometimes, I wonder if I'm leading a jinxed life."

"KA7ITR from KA7ITT."

"KA7ITT from KA7ITR. Go ahead Ann. I'm here with Kim on the dock."

"Patches and I are enroute. Should be there in ten minutes."

Kim and Marc walked back to parking lot area where Captain Gates and Mr. Gressner stood.

"Is that her?" Kim asked as a blue pickup with two antennas on top came down the street.

"Yeah, it is."

They waited while Ann parked and got out. Patches ran immediately to Marc and jumped up to land a slobbery kiss on his face.

"Patches off. Sorry about that Marc — she loves to

kiss people. I've been reluctant to discipline her for it because I don't want to do anything to dampen her friendliness."

Kim was already kneeling down to play with the frisky dog who was returning her greeting with enthusiasm. She stood up and shook hands with Ann. Ann turned to Mr. Gressner.

"I'm so sorry about your son — I just hope we can help."

"I do too."

"How do you want to do this?" Captain Gates asked.

"Where did they come off the ship?"

"Right back there at the gangway area. The kidnapper came down the walkway and from there we're not sure where he went."

"Won't the scents of all the other people who have walked through confuse her?" Mr. Gressner asked.

"It makes it harder but let's see what she can do."

They walked over to edge of the dock. Carefully, making sure that only his protective gloves touched Orlando's sheet, Captain Gates pulled it out onto the ground. Ann pointed to it.

"Patches — here."

The dog obediently sniffed the sheet, even moving part of it with her paw, and pushed it around with her nose.

"Patches — seek!"

Excited, Patches first raised her head and sniffed the air. Then she put her nose to the ground and cast back and forth like a beachcomber with a metal detector. Suddenly near the edge of the dock, her body stiffened and she began moving forward, her nose to the ground.

"Good girl, Patches, seek! Seek!" Ann urged as the dog ran across the parking lot following Orlando's scent. At the sidewalk, she stopped — head raised, bewildered. She put her nose to the pavement, casting around, but each time came up short. Finally she sat down and whined.

"I think this is the end of our trail," Ann said as she looked down at the bright yellow paint on the curb.

"Loading Zone," said Captain Gates. "We may have a lead after all."

He turned to look at the Maritime Museum where Mike Beech, Security Officer, was just emerging, notepad in hand.

****

"Whadya doing?" Mitch asked as Orlando rubbed the smelly foam into his dark hair. "That stuff really stinks, Leo."

"Magical transformation. I've got to be able to move around."

He spread the peroxide mixture thoroughly over his scalp and then sat down to wait per the instructions on the box. It was just one of many things in his bag of tricks that he had carried off the ship. The dark clothing had been left behind in Mitch's first van. Now, dressed in sweatshirt and jeans, Leo Kinelli looked like any resident — almost.

An hour later with his orangish-blond hair trimmed into a ragged crew cut and his moustache, goatee, and side-burns gone, his eyes still had an evil glint to them. He studied himself in the mirror, tried smiling, and finally put on a pair of dark glasses. He flushed his cut hair down the toilet and sent Mitch outside to dispose of the dye bottle in the trash container.

****

To double check the dog's accuracy, Ann took her back to the starting point. This time, they laid an article of Jason's clothing on the ground and commanded her to seek.

Dutifully, Patches nosed the small shirt. She put her nose to the ground and sniffed, but unlike her previous effort, this time she couldn't seem to find any trail. She circled the wooden dock, sniffing both the ground and the air. Finally, she went back to Ann and sat down and whined.

****

For Grant Gressner, the manager of The First Bank of Los Angeles would have opened the branch on Christmas. Gressner's company was one of their largest depositors, and the fact that ninety percent of Computrex's employees also used the bank was an even bigger reason to meet any needs the company's owner might have. But this...

Bank manager Ross Altens felt his own pulse rate quicken as he listened to this bizarre plea from a desperate man. "Three million, Grant! That's impossible."

"It's the only way to save my little boy, Ross."

"Oh Grant. I'm so sorry. Of course, we'll do everything we can to help you. But do the police want you to give this guy the money?"

"Frankly, Ross, I haven't asked their opinion. This is my son whose life I'm trying to save."

His voice rose with emotion, and Ross Altens listened sympathetically to his customer's grief.

"The reason I ask, Grant, is that we had a similar situation once before, except it was the man's wife who was kidnapped. We made up a bag of phony bills and the police caught the guy during the pickup."

"And his wife?"

"She was okay — turned out she was tied up in the trunk of his car."

"Well, there's no car this time, and this is a little boy, my little boy. I want to meet this guy's demands."

"When do you need it?"

"By this evening."

"Wow, listen, that's totally out of the question."

For the next few minutes, Ross Altens attempted to explain to his client why banks no longer carried huge sums of money — that the majority of business was done with checks or electronically. To get that kind of money together, even if it was possible, would mean drawing on every branch office they had plus most likely a trip to the Federal Reserve Bank. It might take a week.

"You've got to get it here by eight tonight, Ross — you've got to. It will take them a little time to get it in the waterproof bag and secured in the right location."

Ross Altens paused. There seemed to be a major point his client was overlooking. Grant Gressner certainly didn't have three million in his personal account. Including their line of credit, there might be that much available in the company's corporate account, but Grant couldn't just transfer that over the phone. He wasn't sure what the company's policy was, but he knew at least two authorized signatures would be needed — maybe even those of the entire Board of Directors.

Grant Gressner was his friend, but so were the other corporate officers of Computrex. If the bank actually could get this money together for Gressner, he, Ross Altens, age 45 and hoping for another twenty years in the banking industry, had jolly well be sure he did it legally. If the money were lost — and who could predict what would happen when you were dealing with criminals? — there was a good chance the company would suffer irreversible losses.

As much as he sympathized with the man on the phone, he wasn't willing to take those losses on himself personally.

"Grant, I know you're upset, but let's back up a minute and go over the procedure for getting this money transferred to your account. Where do you propose taking it from."

There was silence on the line for a minute; then Gressner spoke in a husky voice.

"From the corporate account, Ross. You're not going to throw up a bunch of roadblocks, are you?"

"As few as possible, Grant. But you know you'll need a dual signature to accomplish that. I'll make whatever phone calls you want, but we've got to do this thing properly. We'll take your signature by fax, but the other one has got to be the real thing."

Grant Gressner was barely in control as he answered. "This is my son, we're talking about, Ross — not some set of rules."

"I know, Grant, I know — you want me to set up a conference call, for you?"

"Yeah, I guess — get Jerry Beeman or Andy Simons. One of them ought to be around."

"Okay, give me a phone number where you can be reached."

Grant Gressner gave him not only the motel number but also the police headquarters number off of Captain Gates' card.

"Just remember, Ross; my child's life depends on this."

"I know, Grant. I know."

Ross Altens hung up the phone and sighed. There were a couple of other kidnapping cases he knew about that involved children. In each case, the money was delivered, but the child was dead.

A mental image of the Gressner family with their three blond children hung in his mind. Grant and Amy were so proud of those kids. Ross Altens reached for the phone. First call would be to the Federal Reserve Bank in Portland. If they had the funds, and if Gressner could get the necessary consents, then they could just wire the authorization to make the funds available there. That would save some time.

Chapter 14

South America Dreaming

Tuesday, June 30 11:30 a.m.
Astoria

The license plate of the black van that the guard wrote down belonged to one Brian Mackey — Portland address. It had been stolen one week ago. Mackey had just about given up the hope that it might be recovered. When the squad car pulled up to his house and the officers asked if he owned a 90' Ford Van, he enthusiastically said that he did. Not only did he own it, he was still making payments on it... and it was no fun making payments on something that you no longer even had.

The officers agreed that it wasn't. But unfortunately, they told him, they didn't have his van back. It just was a vehicle of interest in Astoria. Now that they knew where it had last been seen, they would issue an area alert for it.

Captain Gates took this latest information over the phone. He had a hunch that the driver of the van — reported to be in his fifties, graying hair, medium build, was quite possibly involved in the kidnapping. Without a name to track, they were clueless.

"They could be anywhere by now," Mr. Gressner said when Captain Gates told him the news.

"Yes they could, but my feeling is that they're right around here. Somebody has to come back to pick up that ransom money, and believe me, we're going to be waiting for him."

****

"Tell me again about Paraguay, Leo."

Orlando opened a leather pouch and flipped two passports on the bed. One read Samuel Ralston and had a photo of Mitch in it and the other said Frank Hodges and amazingly had a photo of Orlando complete with bleached blond hair.

"How'd you do the hair in the photo?"

"Friend, I found in L.A. You wouldn't believe the stuff they can do with computers these days. After he'd made up yours, I asked him how I'd look as a blond, and he said, 'Like this.' You know I really wasn't sure I wasn't going to color my hair until I saw that photo — looks pretty good, don't you think?"

"Enough about how you look. What about the travel stuff?"

Orlando continued to rummage in his pouch.

"Two tickets to Miami at 9 a.m. tomorrow — two more to Paraguay a day later. Hope you don't mind getting up early."

Mitch snorted.

"Not if you promise I can sleep in the rest of my life. How long we gonna be in Miami?"

"Just overnight. All flights to South America leave in the middle of the day."

"What if there's some hitch, Leo? What if we don't get the money tonight?"

"Relax, I talked to that kid's father — believe me, he'll get the money and he'll get it to us on time."

****

Ross Altens put down the phone. Well, scratch Andy Simons. The Computrex switchboard operator had told him Mr. Simons hadn't come in that day — he had hoped to find him at home. Jerry Beeman had been in some sort of meeting at another plant all morning. Hopefully, he was back in the office by now.

****

12:30 p.m.

Ross Altens could feel his shirt sticking to his back, and he knew it wasn't over 70 degrees in the air-conditioned office. He was waiting on the phone while Robert Stewart of the L.A. Federal Reserve Bank phoned the Federal Reserve Bank in Portland, Oregon on another line to check on availability of funds. He had started to call Portland direct but then stopped as he imagined the conversation. "Hi, I'm Ross Altens from the Los Angeles Bank — Torrance Branch — and we need three million dollars for a ransom — could you kindly tell me if you have that much available today?"

No, there was no graceful way to phrase it. So he called the Federal Reserve Bank in L.A., told the vault manager there (who he did know) a brief summary of what was happening.

"Ross, you still there?"

"Yeah, what's the news, Bob?"

"Normally, they'd have it — no problem, but since it's the 30th, pay day, end of the month, field harvest wages etc., they had tremendous cash draws from their local banks this morning. They'll be getting more funds in later this afternoon. Right now, they've probably only got half your amount."

****

1 p.m.

Jack Herrigan put down the phone. In his twelve year tenure of flying the corporate jet for the Bank of Los Angeles, he'd never had such short notice of a trip. Ross Altens had just phoned him and told him to get the jet ready for possible travel from the Long Beach Airport. Said it was an emergency trip — that hopefully they could work it out by wiring what they needed to Portland, but that there was a possibility that a special cargo was going to have to be flown. He couldn't give him all the details on the phone. Jack flipped open his personal phone book and called Sam Buncie, a mechanic at the hangar where the bank jet along with other planes was stored.

"Yeah, that's right," he told him. "I've got to have her ready to go at a moment's notice, so do all the pre- flight stuff for me, okay? I'll be down there as soon as I hear more."

Jack pulled off his sweatshirt and jeans and put on the khaki trousers and blue denim shirt he liked to fly in. When executives were being ferried somewhere, he added a necktie and a sportcoat to the outfit. For now, he would stay like this. A snag of worry tugged at his stomach. He didn't like the tone of Altens' voice. This was no ordinary mission.

****

"You realize what three million will buy in that country?" Mitch told Orlando as the magician paced back and forth in the motel room. "We'll find ourselves a little place in a green valley near a river — maybe become fishermen or farmers — how about that? Sun, booze, women. "You speak Spanish Leo?"

"Enough. We'll speak money."

"You sure we won't be near the ocean?"

"Nope, but tell you what, Mitch — if you don't like it, after we get ourselves settled as businessmen and all... "

"Wait a minute. I thought we were going to be farmers or fishermen?"

"Just thought of something better. We'll be professional businessmen."

"Doing business in what, Leo?"

"Drugs... that's a great place for it — sort of like being at the top of the food chain, you know. Now get me that wetsuit so I can make sure it fits."

****

The sunlight did little to warm the ground under the Communications Bunker. Deep underground, Jason Gressner lay next to a metal pipe. His head was pushed up against it and he wriggled to move away. The pipe was even colder than the damp soil.

He was done crying. Like a trapped animal, he lay almost still, staring into the darkness. Maybe if he went to sleep, his mommy and daddy would come. He wished he could call to them and tell them where he was, but he couldn't move the gag from his mouth. He tried yelling but the muffled sounds he made scared him even more. And even scarier than that were the chewing sounds he heard. Some sort of creature was eating something near him.

****

It was Lynn, AA7RW, who found the abandoned van. Working in groups of two, the volunteers spread out across the Northwest corner of Oregon searching every road. As they checked each road, they radioed results back to the search coordinator. It didn't take long. At 2 p.m., Lynn working with a friend, found the black van in a thicket of trees near the ocean. The scene was immediately cordoned off and F.B.I. personnel came to dust the van for prints.

After the F.B.I. was done, Ann and Patches were summoned. When asked to seek Jason, the dog unerringly went to the van and stood on the floor in the front seat where the bag had rested.

"Now we don't have the slightest idea what they're driving," Captain Gates said.

****

1:15 p.m.

Ross Altens gave up calling branch offices. Wading through the hierarchy of people and phone waits to find out the vault contents was too time consuming. If this thing were going to work, the money would have to come in big sums — from the Federal Reserve Bank. He still was waiting for Jerry Beeman to call him back; and, reluctantly, following bank protocol, he had put in a call to the Investigative Branch. He'd rather have them know up front what was going on rather than be called on the carpet later.

At 1:27, Beeman phoned him. Ross explained the situation briefly.

"Who do you need to get the required signatures to transfer funds?"

"Wow," was all Jerry Beeman had to say at first. But then he began to think through the situation. "I can't make that decision by myself — let me get a couple of other Board members — we'll be at your office in an hour."

"Okay, I'll have Gressner on the line at that time."

****

Dehydration affects people in different ways. Jason Gressner wasn't in a near death situation... yet, but he was certainly uncomfortable. The gag in his mouth worsened the drying of his mouth and throat. Alone in the dark, he was unaware of hunger, but his throat ached for a cool drink of water.

He closed his eyes and tried to see his parents. He couldn't understand why they didn't come and get him from this scary, cold place. Or why didn't Kim come? He had heard her telling stories at dinner to Reeves family. Once she had rescued her friend Marc. Why didn't she come to save him?

His small hands were tied in front of him and his feet were bound together with some sort of cord that dug into his skin. The man with the gray hair had started to tie his hands behind his back, but Orlando had said, "At least make it so the boy can lie on his back."

By turning on his side, over and over again, he found he could roll across the dirt — but he kept running into that metal pipe that went up the wall. He lay sort of half-curled around the pipe. Now, there was a rock under his side that was cutting into him.

He rolled back until the rock was in grasp of his hands. They felt numb, but he clasped them around it, a small chunk of concrete from one of the inner walls. Still holding the rock, he tried to move beyond the pipe, but his body seemed to be sort of wrapped around it. He couldn't move past the obstacle.

The chewing noises seemed louder. He had to get away. Terrified, he put his tied hands against the pipe and pushed, but he didn't seem to be able to move away from the pipe. He pushed his hands forward desperately. The rock, still in his hand, made a soft clanging noise on the rusty metal.

****

2:30 p.m.

"SJP from ITR."

"Go ahead, Marc."

"Just wondered if there was any word? We're coming back from south 101."

"Nothing yet. The Gressners are waiting to hear from the bank."

"Kim — I've been thinking. Got an idea."

"Anything you want to share on the air?"

"No, I don't think so. I'll be there in ten minutes. Are the F.B.I. people around? I'll need to talk to one of them."

Chapter 15

Behind Closed Doors

Tuesday, June 30th 2:30 p.m.
Los Angeles

T he impromptu Board of Directors meeting for Computrex, Inc. took place at the Torrance Branch of the Los Angeles Bank. Ross Altens closed the heavy mahogany meeting room doors behind him after making sure the phone link with Grant Gressner was established. There was going to be a mass of paperwork to deal with a transfer this size. He had lots to do — assuming the directors would give Gressner his request.

The meeting took place quickly. All the people involved: Grant Gressner, Jerry Beeman, Rebecca Goforth, and Tom Prantis were efficient. Grant Gressner, sounding calmer than he had all day, outlined what he wanted from the group.

As President of the L.A. branch of Computrex, he owned fifty percent of the company. This month's calculation showed the company's net worth at close to twenty-seven million. He was perfectly willing to sign off three million of his share as collateral if the others would authorize the transfer of that amount from the corporate account into his personal account.

It was a unanimous yes vote.

"And we'll say a prayer for Jason, too," added Rebecca Goforth.

But just saying yes wasn't all it took. There were legal papers to draw up. The company attorney was on her way to the bank now. Rebecca Goforth would drive back to the company to get the necessary documents that would be held as collateral for the money. And as soon as the lawyer completed the agreement, it would be faxed to Grant

Gressner who would return a faxed version of the signed document. He would then sign the originals upon his return to Los Angeles. Of course, if the money wasn't lost, it wouldn't be necessary.

****

3:10 p.m.

Grant Gressner hung up the phone with tears in his eyes.

"We got it," he told his wife. "The money's being transferred."

"How?" questioned F.B.I. agent, Phil Lamar. Except for brief interludes, he or Captain Gates had been with the Gressners continuously.

"I'm not sure. It's either being wired to Portland or there's a vague possibility they may fly it up here. Seems the Federal Reserve Bank in Portland is low on cash — won't be getting more until after five."

****

3:20 p.m.

Vera, Ross Altens's secretary, poked her head in the door.

"Sir, the company jet is waiting for you at Long Beach. It's fueled and ready to go."

For the first time that day, the bank manager smiled. "Vera, you're a jewel."

"You think you're going to need it?"

"I don't know yet. I'm hoping we can just do this whole thing by wire, but I'm waiting to hear that they actually have the money there. We're not going to know that until around five or five-thirty."

****

4:30 p.m.

"You got the binoculars?" Orlando questioned Mitch.

"Yeah."

"And the phone number?"

He patted his breast pocket.

"Remember — I won't even begin to suit up until I hear from you that the bag's hanging on the buoy."

"I know, Leo — just relax."

****

5:00 p.m.

"Oh Grant, why doesn't he call?"

"Because he's working right down to the last minute, dear, trying to get the money."

Amy Gressner looked at her watch nervously. The two of them were sitting in the motel room, alternately pacing and staring at the telephone. Julianna and Stacie had left about 3:00 with their grandparents to fly back to San Diego. Kim had just walked out front to wait for Marc driving back from an unsuccessful search.

Captain Gates had excused himself to take a half hour nap back at the station. The two F.B.I. agents were across the street getting some sandwiches. For the moment, the parents of Jason Gressner were all alone. They looked at each other, too tired to even cry any more. Grant reached out and took his wife's hand.

****

5:15 p.m.
Los Angeles

"We've got a major problem," Ross Altens said slamming down the phone. Jerry Beeman, still at the bank after the flurry of paper signing and faxing, listened to the bank manager's explanation.

"Something happened to their Brinks truck — broke down or something an hour ago. It's still waiting for a replacement truck to come and take its load. And all the money is not on board — still has several more stops to make before it will have enough."

"So when will that be?"

"Who knows? Seven, eight? He wasn't even sure he could guarantee the three million."

"How fast can we get it at this end?"

"It's set aside at the Federal Reserve right now. They know we may need it."

Suddenly Jerry Beeman was in control. Not only was Grant the corporation president, but also a good friend whose son they were trying to save.

"Get your pilot to ready the aircraft and then have the money actually delivered to the airport. I'll sign for the bag and be personally responsible for delivering it. Can we fly directly into Astoria?"

"Yes, I believe so."

Ross Altens was on the phone before Jerry Beeman had finished his last sentence. As he waited on hold for the inside line at airport security to answer, he spoke to Beeman.

"I'll arrange everything. Drive on over there now. The security desk is right inside the terminal. Someone will take you onto the runway where the plane will be waiting. The armored truck will come right up to the aircraft."

As Jerry Beeman grabbed his coat and hurried out the door, Ross Altens mouthed the words "Good luck" to him. He looked at the clock. It was 5:30.

****

He didn't know if he could build it that fast, but he would sure give it a try. Marc came out of the radio parts store with a small bag — contents: duct tape, an integrated circuit timer (555), a small "breadboarding" kit, cable, nine volt battery, and a plug. If he could get it all together in time, they might have a way of tracking the money bag. And if they could track the bag, they could catch the kidnapper. Marc climbed into his truck and backed out onto Marine Drive.

****

"Just curious — how'd you get the air tank, Mitch? They won't fill them nowadays unless you have diving certification."

"Yeah, I found that out all right — went into a shop and said I wanted to rent a tank and a suit for my son. No dice on the tank — said the son would have to come in and show those papers you're talking about."

"And?"

"And what?"

"How'd you get it?"

"Just went back that night and took it — there was a bunch of tanks marked filled so I grabbed one and a wetsuit that looked like it might fit and all that other stuff you wanted."

Orlando shook his head.

"So now we've got a hot car, hot diving gear, hot phones — anything else I should know about?"

"How'd you expect me to get it, Leo?"

"Calm down, I'm just weighing our situation here — wondering how many cops out there have a description of you? I know they're all looking for me."

"I wouldn't worry about it — took the stuff from a shop in Portland — this is a long way from there."

Orlando struggled into the wetsuit. It fit — sort of.

He hadn't been diving in twenty years. For a brief period on the outside, he'd attempted to lead a somewhat normal life. Through a Y.M.C.A. in L.A., he'd taken a diving class — done about three open water dives before he got sidetracked robbing stores again.

****

5:55 p.m.

Carrie and Brad Johnson walked out of the historical museum at Fort Stevens. Married just three days ago, they were taking a coastal honeymoon before returning to Eugene next weekend.

"You say your grandfather was stationed here in World War II?" Carrie asked.

"Just for a short time. He trained for an anti aircraft battery and then he shipped out to the Pacific."

"Old Army posts kind of give me a weird feeling — lots of ghosts," Carrie said.

"Yeah, I know. That's the way I was feeling inside the museum looking at all the old uniforms and weapons and stuff."

"So where do you want to go now? Want to spend the night here in Astoria or go across the bridge?"

"Carrie, if you wouldn't mind, I'd kind of like to come back here in the morning for the tour of the bunkers. I was sorry we missed the last one today. Unless, you don't want to?"

She kissed him for an answer and took his hand.

"Let's walk down that road that leads in. We didn't see what was there back of those trees and then let's go back to that crab place we passed in town. Dungeness and lemon butter for dinner."

"You have good ideas," Brad said putting his arm around her and pulling her close.

"So do you," said Carrie.

They walked on companionably, enjoying the late afternoon sunlight filtering through the canopy of trees that overhung the road. Sure enough, when they got about half-way to the entrance of the fort property, a sign pointed off through the trees — "Communication Bunker."

"Did you see that on the map inside, Brad?"

"No, I'm not sure I did. Looks kind of overgrown, doesn't it? I doubt this one is on the tour, but we'll ask about it tomorrow."

They pushed through the branches and climbed up on the aging concrete structure. Carrie sat down and stretched her legs out in a patch of sunlight.

"Don't you want to explore?"

"No, if you don't mind, I'll just sit here and soak up this sunshine."

Brad laughed as she pulled the paperback murder mystery she was reading from her canvas tote bag. Carrie was hopelessly addicted to mysteries.

"You know," he said, "for our honeymoon, we should have gone on one of those 'who dunnit' cruises. I read about them in the paper. You're given clues the first day out and spend the entire cruise trying to solve the murder mystery — would have been right up your alley."

"Mrs. March in the dining room with the candlestick," Carrie laughed. "Maybe on an anniversary sometime — for now I'll just stick with $3.99 paperbacks. Go on — go explore."

"You just want to get rid of me," Brad said with a mock pout. But he was already climbing up some steps to a higher level of the bunker.

Carrie smiled and stretched luxuriously in the sun. Just twenty pages more to go. If she read fast, maybe she would find out "who dunnit" before he got back.

She turned the last page just as he came back and sat down beside her.

"Happy?" he asked.

"Very... did you hear that?"

"What?"

"I don't know — sort of a thump down below us and kind of like a kitten meowing."

"I don't hear anything. Maybe you're just imagining it. Or maybe," he said, lowering his voice dramatically, "it's a mystery — the ghost of some entrapped pirate who wants out of the bunker. Ooooh."

"Let's get one thing straight, Brad Johnson, my dearly beloved husband of three days — I do not imagine things."

"Do you still hear it, dearly beloved wife of three days who doesn't imagine things?"

"No, I don't and don't make fun of me."

"I'm not, I'm not!"

At that, the two of them started tickling each other and laughing. In a few minutes, they climbed down from the bunker and made their way back to the car, holding hands.

****

6:10 p.m.

The Falcon Jet taxied out on the runway. Co-pilot Rich Meeks turned and looked at their sole passenger, Jerry Beeman. Seat belted into the first seat behind them, he sat anxiously staring out the window, a huge canvas bag at his feet.

Chapter 16

Deadlines

Tuesday, June 30th 6:30 p.m.
Astoria

K im greeted Marc with a kiss outside the motel.
"Any news?" he asked.
"Yeah, they just got a call. The money's not going
to work out in Portland, so they're actually flying it here.
Took off from Long Beach fifteen minutes ago."

Marc glanced at his watch and whistled.

"Think they'll make it?"

"The Gressners are still hopeful, but I can tell the
F.B.I. guys and Captain Gates don't think so. They're already telling Mr. Gressner what to say if the kidnapper calls
when the deadline isn't met."

Marc was walking toward the motel as Kim talked.

"What's your idea you mentioned?"

"I'll show you. Is there a place where I can work —
like a table or something?"

"Sure. Maybe in one of the rooms the F.B.I. agents
are using. Let's ask."

Kim knocked gently on the Gressner's motel room
door and Captain Gates answered it. He smiled at the young
couple who were impressing him more each hour with their
calm efficiency in this increasingly stressful situation.

"Sir," Marc began. "I have an idea of a way to track
the money. What kind of a bag is it going to be in?"

"Canvas, I believe. We've got an outer waterproof
sealer to tie it in once it gets here. That's what the kidnapper requested."

Marc held up the small paper sack of radio parts
and removed his micro-miniature transceiver from his shirt
pocket. It was the tiniest model available — purchased

just two months ago as the result of some unexpected money he earned playing with his band at fraternity dances. The idea of putting it where it could get wet... he swallowed and explained what he planned to do.

"I've got the stuff to make a simple integrated circuit timer to key this radio. It will automatically put the rig into transmit mode for five seconds and then back into receive for thirty seconds. If we slip the radio into the bag, we should be able to get a bearing on its location once every thirty-five seconds. And as you know, we've got a lot of hams here more than willing to help track him."

Captain Gates's face showed his approval.

"Why not just have it transmit all the time?"

"Couple of reasons. It saves battery power this way, and maybe you'll want to transmit to the kidnapper."

Captain Gates raised his eyebrows at this suggestion.

"I just wanted to leave that possibility open, sir."

"Let's get you a place to work, son."

****

6:45 p.m.

"Okay?"

"Yeah — pull down in that clump of trees."

Watching his rearview mirror to make sure no one was behind him, Mitch eased off the highway onto a gravel road that led down to the water. Orlando sat next to him, nervously fingering the tight bundle of clothing in his lap. A pair of tennis shoes, jeans, and shirt were wrapped around one of the three cellular phones. Now to hide it.

They parked behind a sprawling clump of blackberries.

"Wait here," Orlando told Mitch.

Moving quickly, he hiked along the edge of the rocky shore access along the Columbia River. Shading his eyes with his hand, Orlando scanned the hillside behind him.

There... farther up on the hill was a yellow light — probably a porch or garage light attached to the house partially shielded by shore pine. That would be his landmark.

Orlando cast around for a sheltered area. Nothing right next to the water. He settled for some taller sedge grass growing among uneven boulders that made up the slanting shore line. Carefully, he wedged his package under one of the rocks. He looked left and right to get his bearings — shouldn't be too hard to find — even in the dark. Scrambling over the slippery rocks, he ran back up to rejoin Mitch.

****

7:00 p.m.

Captain Gates stood in the parking lot of the deserted cannery. He turned to one of his deputies.

"When will they be here?"

"At 7:30. Just tell me where you want them positioned, and I'll get everyone in place."

"Let's put a couple up under the trestle, one upstairs in the cannery, two by the road — get someone up at the point so we can see anything coming from the east, and maybe two more down by the Coast Guard. Coast Guard personnel have a boat ready to go down at the station — if we can find a place to hide it, they may bring a runabout up here. We've got to be completely under cover though."

"How do we know the guy's not watching us right now?"

"We don't and realistically, he's got to know the police are involved. My guess is that he's going to pick the money up in some sort of high speed craft. He knows we won't overtly chase him because the kid's life is at stake. At night, I imagine he thinks he can just disappear."

"What do you think?"

"About his disappearing? It's going to be hard to keep him in sight without being seen, but we've got a sharp college kid building some sort of tracking device for us right now — let's hope it works."

****

7:15 p.m.

Co-pilot Rich Meeks turned to look back at their sole passenger.

"You doing okay back there?"

"I'm fine. Where are we?"

"Almost to Sacramento."

Jerry Beeman stared at his watch for perhaps the hundredth time that evening.

"Shouldn't we be farther along?"

"Headwind slowing us down some and there are some thunderheads up across the border. We may be slowed even more."

"So when do you think we'll reach Astoria?"

"Realistically? About 8:45 — maybe even 9:00."

"Can you radio that information ahead?"

"We already have. There's no tower at Astoria, but Air Control at Seattle has been forwarding our estimated arrival time to the police in Astoria."

****

7:30 p.m.

Kim stood a little to the side of Marc watching him work.

"Anything I can do?"

"Thanks, but I guess one pair of hands is all that can fit onto the board. Just keep me company and think good thoughts."

Kim sat down at the small motel table watching her friend work. She always got a kick out of the way Marc talked his way through problems. Even though his eyes were intently focused on the circuit he was building, his voice could have been that of a college professor.

"If we make the timer parallel with the push to talk, then..."

His brow furrowed as he finished wiring the device to his transceiver. Complete with the short "rubber duck" antenna, the entire unit was about half the size of a pack of cigarettes.

"Here," he said, handing it to Kim. "Give me your rig and walk outside with this one. Don't do anything to it — just carry it."

Kim held it in the palm of her hand and walked out the door. One of the F.B.I. agents was standing on the pathway to the motel, talking on his cellular phone. Apparently, he'd just finished a conversation because he stuck the phone back in his pocket and walked over to see what she was doing.

She held out her hand to show him the transceiver. The little red transmit light was on indicating the output signal was initiated.

"One, two, three, four, five." Kim counted aloud. At "five," the light went off.

"KA7SJP from KA7ITR — this is a test."

The voice was clearly audible through the tiny receiver. Kim turned and waved at Marc who was standing in the doorway watching. At thirty seconds, the transmit light went back on.

"Just tell us where you want the ham radio operators to wait and they'll begin tracking the minute the bag's picked up," Kim told the agent.

He nodded but then looked at his watch.

"If it is picked up... right now, we've got a major time problem."

****

7:45 p.m.

Mitch pulled the van over to the curb in the residential neighborhood high on the bluff above the ocean. It was starting to rain so the streets were almost vacant. One woman walking a dog passed him on the sidewalk as he strolled down to the park at the end of the street. He had been here before and he knew where he wanted to go.

He waited until the woman turned the corner and then walked rapidly down the path that led to a grove of fir trees. Just beyond the trees was a rocky slope, heavily overgrown with pines and blackberries. It was the perfect place to wait and watch the buoy with binoculars. In just about an hour, the action should begin.

****

8:15p.m.

"Oh no," Amy Gressner sobbed when the phone call came. The Falcon jet carrying the ransom was over Eugene, Oregon. Expected touchdown was at 8:45. Even if they were waiting with the waterproof bag at the airport, it wasn't going to work.

"Figure five minutes to get the bag arranged, ten minutes to get down to the water, ten more to get it out to the buoy and secured, five to ten more for the unexpected," Captain Gates said.

"Unexpected!" Amy cried.

"We're not exactly sure of their landing time," the captain told her gently.

"But won't the kidnapper wait?"

"We don't know what he's going to do, Mrs. Gressner. At 8:30, we're going to take you and your husband along with one of the F.B.I. agents to the phone booth down at the pavilion."

She was too distraught to answer.

****

8:30 p.m.

It was hot in the wetsuit, and Orlando was sweating even though he'd just put it on a few minutes ago. He was hidden in shrubbery right at the shoreline about one quarter mile east of the buoy. Mitch had dropped him off before going up to his surveillance point on the bluff.

Fortunately, this was on the edge of an isolated lagoon, and he didn't think anyone had noticed him as he'd made his way down the trail, carrying his heavy bag of diving gear. In a little over an hour, he hoped to be carrying an equally heavy bag of money up a different trail farther up the river.

It was high tide which meant he'd have to swim against the current on his way down to the buoy. But he'd have his air tank on for that. On the way back, swimming with the current, he planned to jettison the tank and just snorkel under the surface. He'd made sure there was no orange stripe on the snorkel. With the rain, it was already pretty dark. Maybe they should have scheduled this whole thing earlier.

Chapter 17

Touchdown

Tuesday, June 30th 9 p.m.
Astoria

F B.I. agent Phil Lamar and Sheriff's deputy David
Heilly watched the sleek Falcon jet splash through
the water on the runway. What had started as
sprinkles was now a steady rain. Heilly looked at his watch
— 9:01.

Marc Lawrence sat in the back seat of the car, the
empty waterproof money bag beside him. In his hand was
the transceiver he had just finished adapting. He turned it
over, carefully examining it to make sure that his taped as-
sembly was securely in place.

Lamar was at the wheel of their unmarked car. He
waited until the aircraft made its turn to taxi toward the
small air terminal before starting the car engine. Looking
left and right, he eased out onto the runway.

****

"They're there," Jerry Beeman, Vice President of
Computrex, Inc., said aloud, just to himself. He gripped
the money bag, prepared to move as quickly as possible
once the plane stopped.

****

9:05 p.m.

Everything was ready at the buoy site. Law enforcement officers flattened into the dark landscape — under
the train trestle, behind rocks, under shrubs — their binoculars focused on the buoy and the surrounding water.
Everything was ready except for the money. Sheriff's

deputy Rich Cambria turned to his partner. They had just received word that the plane had landed. The money was being transferred now.

"It's going to be at least nine twenty — probably nine twenty-five before that money's in place. I wonder if we're dealing with a patient kidnapper."

His partner kind of half-smiled.

"Dealing. You really think we should be 'dealing?' with a kidnapper."

"It's the guy's kid. Can't blame him for that."

"No, I guess not. Wonder why the kidnapper picked three million. I mean, how do you put a price on a kid?"

****

9:10 p.m.

Amy Gressner clung fiercely to her husband's arm. F.B.I. Agent Tim Matheson had pulled his squad car right up to the phone booth so they could sit out of the rain. But both Amy and Grant preferred to stand next to the phone itself.

Kim sat quietly in the back of the car. She held her tiny two meter radio to her ear. The ham radio operators of Astoria and the surrounding area were ready to move into action. Once Marc gave them the message that the signal had been activated on 146.535 simplex, they would be listening, ready to track the man who had taken a helpless child.

Matheson watched the Gressners sympathetically. He had been trying to coach them as to what to say when and if the kidnapper called, but in the end it would be their choice of words. The phone company had fully cooperated in initializing a trace from the phone booth, but everyone involved expected the call to come from a cellular phone as had the others.

As the rain poured down, the Gressners squeezed inside the phone booth. Matheson thought of other kidnapping investigations he had been involved in and then he thought about his own twin six year old boys at home. Grant and Amy Gressner looked much older to him than they had this morning. The digital clock on his dash read 9:12. p.m.

****
9:15 p.m.

For a while in the afternoon, Jason's terror had subsided. The rock in his hand gave him something to hold and being able to hit it against the pipe and make a noise broke through the isolation barrier that separated him from all that he knew. He tapped a few times against the pipe. He liked the ringing sound it made — kind of like when Kim had tapped code to him on the railing of the ship.

It was a fun game they had played. He'd sat on the deck, his ear pressed next to the pipe, and she had tapped letters against the pipe a few feet away. He had yelled them out as he heard them. Afterwards, they had all gone up on the Sun Deck for ice cream.

Dit dit dit dah dah dah dit dit dit — that was what Kim said people should send in code if they were in trouble. He tapped the rock against the pipe. Then his arms hurt and he felt cold. He put his head down on the damp soil and went to sleep.

****
9:20 p.m.

Jerry Beeman and F.B.I. Agent Lamar worked frantically stuffing the money bag into the waterproof plastic casing. It was a tight fit. Lamar had switched places with the sheriff's deputy so he could drive while they manipulated the bags. Just as they approached the coastline, the transfer was complete. Marc handed Lamar the transceiver.

"Does it matter where?"

"Not really," Marc told him. "Don't you suppose they'll open the bag and look in? Let's hide this way in the bottom."

Lamar held the bulging bag open with both his hands. Three hundred bundles of money, each one containing ten thousand dollars in hundred dollar bills, were stacked neatly inside. Marc pushed his left hand down the inside edge, creating a hollow space at the bottom and then shoved the transceiver into it, making sure everything was still intact and that the rubber ducky antenna was next to the fabric.

Now they were at the shoreline. A small Coast Guard runabout stood ready, its engine running. The time was 9:26.

The men got out of the car and ran to it.

****

9:27 p.m.

"Money's in place. They're taking it out now," Agent Matheson relayed to the Gressners as the message came over his radio."

Grant Gressner put his arm around his wife in the cramped area of the phone booth, and she leaned her face against his chest.

****

9:28 p.m.

"They're there," Mitch hissed into his cellular phone.

"Too late. I'm not going out there in pitch black. Water's so rough with this storm — take me an hour just to swim down there."

"You sure?"

"Yeah, Mitch, I'm sure. Don't panic — same time tomorrow, but first I got to call those folks and scare them into better service.

****

Thirteen vehicles equipped with direction finding antennas were parked at strategic locations near the designated drop zone. In the drivers' seats were thirteen dedicated Amateur Radio operators listening to the emergency net underway on two meters. The transceiver in the money bag had just been activated. Several more "hams" were standing ready at the Coast Guard Station in case their services were needed on board chase vessels. Nobody knew what the kidnapper's plans were — whether he would have the child with him — whether he would be alone or with an accomplice.

Law enforcement officials had given all the volunteers strict instructions. Everyone was to stay out of sight and no one was to try to apprehend. The man was not to suspect that he was being followed. He had made it quite clear to the Gressners that if police trailed him, that Jason would die.

****

9:30 p.m.

"Hello!"

Grant Gressner grabbed the phone before it was even a second into its ring. Kim felt her stomach knot as she watched and heard his end of the conversation. His face turned red and she could tell that his anxiety was being replaced with anger.

"I told you it was impossible to raise that much money in a day. You have no idea what it took to get it here."

His voice became a shout.

"What do you mean you want to wait until tomorrow! I want my son back and I want him now!

Amy reached out to touch her husband, but he pushed her hand away.

"Listen you creep and listen good. I'm not going to go through with this at all unless I talk to Jason again. You put him on the phone NOW!"

Kim could tell the F.B.I. agent was worried about Grant Gressner's responses too because he got out of the car and shook his head warningly at him through the window. But Jason's father was on a roll. All the sorrow and tension of the last twenty-four hours was coming out.

"Look, I'm telling you — go get him and put him on the line. What do you mean, he's not there? No, NO! You listen to me. I'm not going to stand out here all night. I'm going to go back to my room at the Sea Edge Motel. You get Jason and you phone me there and then we'll talk about the pickup for tomorrow."

Kim watched in amazement as he slammed the phone down. He turned toward his wife, the color slowly draining from his face, and gathered her into his arms. Agent Matheson pulled out his two way radio and spoke into it quietly.

"Another cellular call, but a different number. We're investigating it," he said.

He waited patiently for Gressner to regain his composure. Shuddering with emotion, the distraught father related Orlando's side of the conversation.

"He said he was calling it off for tonight—too dark and stormy, he said. Why would that make a difference? Seems like if they're trying to make a getaway in a boat, that would be to their advantage. And you heard what I said. He said Jason wasn't right there — that I couldn't talk to him. I'm sure he's dead…"

His voice broke into sobs and Matheson put a hand on his shoulder.

"Let's get you folks back to the motel," he said gruffly.

****

9:45 p.m.

"It's off," Captain Gates said, clipping his radio back on his belt. "Bring it back in."

The Coast Guardsmen pushed their boat out of its hiding place and started the engine.

****

10 p.m.

Cursing as he dressed, Orlando wriggled out of the clammy wetsuit and stuffed it back in his diving bag. The rain was pelting down now and he shivered as he struggled into his jeans and cotton shirt. He pulled the phone out of his bag.

"Okay, come get me . I'll be at the road in two minutes."

Chapter 18

Night Calls

Tuesday, June 30th 10:30 p.m.
Astoria

"He's dead, I know he's dead," Amy Gressner said tearfully.

Kim stood against the wall, not knowing what to do or say. There were so many people crowded into the room, one of the sheriff's deputies had brought in extra chairs.

The Gressners sat together on the bed. Grant Gressner kept staring at the phone on the maple table next to the television.

"I shouldn't have hung up on him," he said quietly.

"No sir," F.B.I. agent Phil Lamar reassured him. "I think that was good. It lets him know you're not a victim — that you're someone to be dealt with. The farther we can push him into complying with your demands, the better chance we have of catching him."

"But what about Jason?"

"Just wait and see. I wouldn't be surprised if the kidnapper calls back. Don't second guess anything. Just play this thing hour by hour. It's the only way you're going to get through it."

For a brief second, Lamar exchanged glances with DeputyDavid Heilly who was standing in the doorway. Kim caught the interchange and knew instantly that neither Heilly nor Lamar believed Jason was alive. She got up and slipped past Heilly outside under the covered walkway. Marc was talking to one of the sheriff's deputies. They had just come back from depositing the money bag (the transceiver turned off to save batteries) in the vault at the sheriff's office.

Marc raised his eyebrows questioningly as Kim came over to him.

"Looks like it's stopped raining," she said gesturing out at the still night where moonlight was beginning to silver through parting clouds.

Marc sighed and put his arm around Kim. She would only talk about the weather when there was nothing else to say.

"Yeah," he agreed.

"You kids have a place to stay?" the deputy asked.

"I'm at the Jensens just up the road. I'm sure they've got room for you too, Kim if you want."

Kim looked tempted but she shook her head.

"I guess I should stay here with the Gressners — they've got two rooms. I'm not sure what I can do for them, but if there's anything, I want to be available."

"So what's happening in there?" Marc asked. "Are they going to try the drop again tomorrow night?"

"I don't know — I guess they'll decide that tomorrow. The F.B.I. guys are telling them to just take it hour by hour. Jason's mother is sure he's dead."

"What do you think, Kim?"

"Oh... I don't know, Marc."

She turned away as tears filled her eyes.

****

10:45 p.m.

"He wants to talk to him?"

They were driving east toward Portland simply because Mitch couldn't think of any other place to go. The headlights of passing cars flashed over his angry face.

"I told you one day wasn't enough time to get that kind of money, but noooo, you said they could do it. Now what have we got? Every cop in the state looking for us and not a dime to our names."

"Back off, Mitch. This is gonna work. I just gotta think about it."

"Well don't think about going back to the fort to that kid."

"You're the one who picked that location."

"That's right and it's a fine place to leave a kid."

"As long as we don't need to go there, right?"

"Right," agreed Mitch.

They drove on in the night, finally stopping in Vernonia at a small motel. Orlando agreed that Mitch's place might be under surveillance.

"You think they know you're in on this by now?"

"Oh, maybe not, considering the phones which they may have traced were stolen...

"Stolen?"

"Yeah, stolen. What do you think I am Leo — the Prince of Wales or something? Same problem as I had with the scuba gear — there you had to have a certification card. At the phone store, you had to have a credit card to activate an account. And you think I'd want an account in my name? The first call I made, they'd be on my doorstep. Once they're on my doorstep, they'd be inside my place. I'm funny that way, Leo. I don't want anyone messing around in my stuff... even if I'm not ever going back to it."

"The phones are stolen — right?"

"Leo, you are just too bright for words."

Orlando's brow wrinkled with anger. He'd forgotten how Mitch enjoyed putting people down. Still he listened to his explanation.

"So I got these phones through a friend. That's why I showed you how to access a different base number every time we use the phone. If the calls are being traced, and I'm ninety-nine percent sure they are, each one may be shut down after we make a call."

"How many numbers you got there, Mitch?"

"Twelve — how many calls you gonna make."

"Just eleven. I'll save the last one so you can call Santa."

"That's good, Leo. You may not be too bad to live with after all."

"Okay, back to the original question. Nobody should know who you are — right?"

"The only one I'm worried about is that security guard in Astoria who seemed a little too interested in me — let's just not take any chances."

****

Wednesday July 1st 1:30 a.m

Amy Gessner sat bolt upright in bed when the phone rang. Even as Grant reached for it, he knew that the line which had been linked to an adjacent room occupied by the F.B.I. agents was being monitored.

"Hello?" he said hesitantly.

Orlando's voice was so loud and husky that Amy could hear it three feet away. She clutched the pillow to her for comfort as her husband attempted a conversation with the kidnapper.

"You listen to me this time, Mr. Rich Man. I wasn't gonna call you at all but I thought I'd level with you. The reason you can't talk to your kid is because he isn't with me where I am — and where he is you got the whole town crawling with police. You think I don't know that, but I do."

Jason's father tried to speak, but Orlando bulldozed right over him.

"You shut up mister. Just listen to me. Your kid's okay. You hang that money on the buoy and keep the cops away after I pick it up and you'll get your kid back — if not, well then I guess that's your choice. Let's make it eight o'clock tonight so we can all get to bed early."

There was a click and then a buzzing dial tone. Within seconds, Agent Lamar was knocking on the door.

Exhausted as she was, Kim managed to sleep through the ringing phone, but for some reason, the knock on the Gressner's door thrust her awake. She grabbed her robe and cracked open the adjoining door to their room. Amy motioned her in.

"You think there's any chance he's still alive?" Grant asked the agent.

"Like I said, let's just take this thing hour by hour."

It took almost an hour before Portland police located the registered owners of the cell phone number Orlando had called on. Like the two before them, they turned out to be innocent victims of a criminal who was using the wonders of communication technology for his own evil doing.

****

3 a.m.

At the Jensen household, Ann crept quietly out of bed, careful not to waken her husband. She tiptoed past her son's bedroom where Marc was — asleep she hoped. There was a small light over the kitchen stove which she turned on. The soft jingle of dog tags made her turn around and smile.

"Nobody sneaks past you, do they, Patches?"

The dog sat down and opened her mouth in a tremendous yawn.

"Yeah, I know, it's a little early, but I just couldn't sleep."

She sat down on a kitchen stool and scratched the dog's ears affectionately while talking to her.

"A long time ago — in fact about twenty years before you were born — our boys were about the size of that little Jason who's missing. I keep thinking about them — how small and vulnerable they were and how scared they would have been if someone had taken them away."

Patches whined and licked Ann's hand. Ann picked up her handheld radio and checked into the net.

****

3:10 a.m.

Orlando lay awake in the uncomfortable motel bed and listened to Mitch snore. So they weren't going to go back for the kid. Big deal, he told himself. They were going to get three million for this job. They were going to be rich for the rest of their lives.

He thought back over the crimes he had committed. It was kind of hard to bring them all into focus. One burglary ran into another. Two big robberies — one of a liquor store and the other of a small grocery had landed him in jail. In the grocery store attempt — which had failed, he had shot the store owner. The owner recovered and identified him in a line-up the following month when he was arrested in another hold-up attempt. He'd had no particular feelings about shooting that guy. If he hadn't lived, then he might not have been arrested. But Leo Kinelli had never killed a child. Not until now.

****

5 a.m.

There was no difference in the darkness in the bunker, night or day. Now disoriented as to time of day, Jason knew only that there was a bad time. That was when the chewing and scurrying noises got louder and louder. The creatures were ripping apart something. He had heard them draw close to him and felt their tiny feet running across his legs.

It scared him beyond any fear that he had ever known — more than the dark — more than the memory of Orlando's face.

He tried making noise, whimpering behind his gag, but the soft mewing sound he was able to utter only seemed to attract them. He clenched his small fingers around the rock he'd held through the night.

He rocked his small body near the pipe and began to tap against it with the rock. The echoing hollow noise seemed to drive the creatures back. Jason kept the cadence going. GO AWAY, he said over and over in his head to the beat of the repeated triads of dits and dahs.

Finally, he fell asleep, his tiny face resting against the pipe. What woke him was a new noise. For a few terrified minutes, his ears sought out the night noises, but they were gone. He pressed his ear closer to the pipe and heard a faint twittering noise. For some reason the sound made him a little less terrified.

****

5:05 a.m.

The sun's rising glow extended through the trees that shaded the drive leading into Fort Stevens. And with the golden ascent that cast its light through the lush green trees, the birds began to sing in earnest.

Chapter 19

Leads and Dead Ends

Wednesday, July 1st 6:00 a.m.
Astoria

Orlando had finally gone to sleep about 4:00 a.m. As Mitch lay on his side watching his partner slumbering, he felt his anger rise. This one basic detail — how long it would take to raise ransom money — left the the whole scheme in jeopardy.

The plan, carefully plotted in the prison yard at the Oregon State Penitentiary, had been developed over a period of months. Believing that they were equals, Mitch had accepted the arbitrary division of tasks that Leo had laid out.

He shook his head as he thought about Leo wanting to go back to the kid in the middle of the night. He was actually going to deal with the parents — accept their demands. It was obvious that somebody needed to take charge of this operation or the whole thing would go down the drain and they would be back in prison. This time, the term would be life, or if the kid died... he sat up and grabbed a shirt.

Mitch slipped out of bed. He really didn't think anyone knew he was involved with this... yet. The only way of checking it out would be to get the morning paper. He finished dressing quickly and closed the door behind him.

It was a short walk to a corner cafe where locals were drinking coffee. Mitch didn't go in — just put coins in the paper machine on the sidewalk. He scanned the front pages as he walked back to the motel.

Mitch waved the paper at Orlando as he opened the door. Orlando blinked as the light hit his eyes. He gestured toward the paper questioningly.

"Nothing yet but they may be keeping it quiet."

****

6:30 a.m.

Captain Gates also breathed a sigh of relief as he read all the papers available. Unbelievably, this thing hadn't leaked to the press yet, but he knew that would change today.

In fact, he'd already had a call that a reporter was waiting for him back at the office.

He was more interested in information that was coming in from the Oregon State Penitentiary. At the F.B.I.'s request, personnel there had worked up a file, trying to piece together what they knew about Orlando. So far it was sketchy, but they were awaiting more information.

Leo Kinelli "Orlando" had been born in 1948 to Roseanna and Vincent Kinelli in Chicago, Illinois. Vincent Kinelli a machinist in an auto parts manufacturing plant, had died in a car accident two years after Leo's birth.

Leo had no siblings. All of this personal information was coming from Mary Ann Stesson, his divorced wife. She had been married to him for two years 1967-69 in Green Bay Wisconsin. That was where he pulled his first job (robbery of a gas station) that landed him in the Wisconsin State Prison for a year. It also ended his marriage. That information had been forwarded to the warden at Oregon who phoned Green Bay to see if by any chance Mary Ann Stesson still lived there and was listed in the phone directory.

Yes on both counts. She sounded almost wistful as she recounted her memory of the tall dark man she had fallen in love with. He had just been getting ready to go in the Army when he robbed the station. She guessed she had really never known him — hadn't a clue that he would do something like that. She divorced him while he was still in prison.

His life history from there read like a checkerboard. Good years interspersed with bad ones. His cleanest time had been from 1978-1981 when he'd worked as a ranch hand in Montana. Then for some reason, he'd drifted away to Oregon and had started robbing stores — first little jobs and then bigger ones. The shooting incident landed him back in prison.

As far as the warden knew, there had been no other marriages and no children. Leo Kinelli had not been a bad prisoner. He was somewhat of a loner but he'd had one special buddy — a guy named Mitch Foler. Foler was sixty-one now — had been released six months ago. The two of them used to walk the yard together, and later on when they were assigned to a work detail together, they'd planted the rows and rows and marigolds that bordered the prison driveway on State Street. The warden was gathering data on Foler and would send it on as soon as it was compiled.

****
9:00 a.m.

Captain Gates stood outside on the walkway, chatting with agent Phil Lamar. He held the printed sheets that had been faxed to him about Orlando.

"We're trying to get a recent address on his buddy — name of Mitch Foler. Looks like he's moved three, maybe four times since he got out."

Sitting on the brick planter that bordered the lawn, Kim sipped a cup of tea. She was rehashing everything that had happened. Orlando couldn't have done this all by himself. He would have needed somebody on board to help him — wouldn't he?

Suddenly, a vision of Ferdy, their waiter, flashed through her mind. Ferdy making friends with Jason. Ferdy recommending the magic show. Ferdy avoiding eye contact the morning after.

I'm probably imagining things, Kim told herself, but the kidnapping was very real. She'd had bad vibes about Orlando and not shared them. This time she wasn't keeping anything to herself.

"Excuse me," she said standing up. "It's probably nothing, but you might want to do some checking on the waiter we had — name was Ferdy."

****

11:00 a.m.

"You sure you don't want to go with me?"

"No honey, I guess there are some things you don't know about me. One of them is that I have claustrophobia. The thought of being in those underground bunkers just kind of makes me feel sick thinking about it."

"I guess I'll be gone about an hour."

"Don't worry. I can keep busy."

Carrie pulled another murder mystery from her bag, and Brad laughed. The rain of last night had completely cleared and Carrie strolled across the grounds admiring the plantings. On an impulse, she headed back down the drive where the two of them had explored yesterday.

It felt good to walk in the sun, and she pulled off her sweat shirt as she walked and tied it around her waist. The Communications Bunker was a ten minute walk from where she'd left Brad at the museum. Slinging her canvas purse over her shoulder, she climbed up on the concrete structure and stretched out in the sunshine with her book.

Down below her, one very small exhausted boy slept, his body fighting bravely to stay alive.

****

Noon

Captain Dirilica listened carefully as Captain Gates talked to him on the ship to shore telephone.

"I've got his personnel records right here. The only Ferdinand we have has the last name of Simington. He came to work for us in '92. He lists some work experience — not extensive. The guy's only twenty-seven. Been a good employee as far as I can tell — possibly drinks too much when

146

he's off duty but there's never been a problem on board."

"Would you question him please?"

1 p.m.

Seattle

The Sea Mystic was busy taking on supplies for its return voyage to Ensenada. Most of the passengers had gone ashore but some had stayed on board to enjoy the shipboard activities. Ferdy was carrying a tray of sandwiches to the late buffet when the ship's first officer came to tell him the Captain wanted to see him on the Bridge. Ferdy dropped the tray. Desperately, he tried to wipe any expression of fear from his face as he followed the first officer up the stairwells.

In a small room off the Bridge, Captain Dirilica questioned his waiter rather harshly. He had no idea whether the man was innocent or guilty but there was something in his face that made him suspicious.

"What was your association with the magician?" he asked him repeatedly over the next hour.

Ferdy just kept shaking his head.

"I saw him around — just like everybody else. Other than that I don't know anything about him."

A deepening flush of red crept up Ferdy's neck at each question, but he hesitated only a second before answering.

"How well did you get to know the Gressner family at your table?"

Finally, the inquisition was over and Ferdy was allowed to go back to work.

"You notice something?" the captain said to the first officer after the waiter had left.

"Yeah. He never once asked why he was being questioned or what had happened with Orlando. Seems kind of odd, doesn't it?"

"Very odd. I've called our central office to get more information on him. For the meantime, since we're in port, I want someone watching him to make sure he doesn't try to leave."

Chapter 20

The Longest Day

Wednesday, July 1st. 2 p.m.
Astoria

There wasn't much for the Gressners to do to occupy their day. At Captain Gates' insistence, they took turns away from their phone vigil while each of them lay down for a short nap.

Amy Gressner talked to Julianna and Stacie on another phone line in Kim's room. They were fine. Grandma and Grandpa were taking good care of them... but when would they get Jason back? Amy couldn't answer them.

****

3 p.m.

It was the first time Kim and Marc had been alone all day. Kim had stayed with Amy, getting her tea and encouraging her to eat a sandwich at noon. Marc had attended an organizational meeting of volunteer ham radio operators who would be attempting to track the kidnapper if the ransom delivery went through as planned.

"The sheriff's deputy who talked to us was certainly emphatic," Marc told Kim.

"What did he say?"

"Oh, he talked about the importance of our involvement being for tracking only. Said that those working with the Coast Guard would be under their direction."

"You think the pickup's going to be by boat? That's what the Gressners believe."

"Yeah, he said that was the most likely scenario. The guy will pick up the money in a boat, go a ways either up or down the shore line and then get into a vehicle. We're supposed to make sure no one interferes with him."

Marc paused.

"He also said that they don't believe a word the kidnapper has said about calling with the child's whereabouts, but until they're certain that he's not going to do that, nobody is to impede his progress."

Kim looked at her watch.

"Long day."

"Yeah," Marc agreed.

****

3:30 p.m.

The phone rang in the F.B.I. agents' room and Lamar answered. It was Captain Dirilica. Ferdy had just been caught trying to sneak off the ship. He was being intensely interrogated now.

****

4:00 p.m.

Mitch and Orlando had been in town for an hour. They stopped at a grocery halfway between Vernonia and Astoria and picked up a few food items. From a pay phone, Orlando called the airline and asked what the chances were they could go standby on a "red-eye" flight to Miami that night. No problem, he was told. It looked wide open. Just be sure to check in by midnight.

They stashed the diving gear and the extra set of clothes and phone and then drove down a logging road to hang out for a while. There was just one more errand to run. Even with Orlando's new orange-blonde hair, Mitch decided it was safer if he made the trip.

****

4:15 p.m.

"He confessed," Agent Phil Lamar told the Gressners. Captain Gates had gone back to the station to catch a little sleep before tonight's events.

"When the authorities told this Ferdy guy they knew all about Leo Kinelli and his buddy Mitch, he just sort of came unglued."

Grant Gressner listened attentively.

"And there's probably more to this story than we know yet. Ferdy apparently started crying during this whole questioning bit — kept saying something about not meaning to kill Orlando. Then he stopped talking all together, but they'll keep after him."

"Kill Orlando? That doesn't even make sense. Did he say anything about where they were going to hide Jason?" Amy Gressner pleaded.

"Not that he would tell us, but as I said, they're just getting started with him."

****

6:30 p.m.

"Hi honey. Yeah I just got back. Pretty good run today. Everything okay?"

Standing outside at the pay phone in the Astoria Marina, Jon Adams listened to his wife tell about the day's events. She had dinner in the oven — would he be home soon?

"No, listen, I've got to unload here and clean everything up for tomorrow, but I do have some good news besides the fantastic salmon haul we had today. Seems they're filming some sort of television commercial here tonight. I guess it has to do with the magic festival. A guy just gave me $500. All I have to do is run the boat up past town and circle a buoy while they film. When I get back, he said he'd be here with another $500."

He smiled as he listened to her exclamation and then her motherly advice to wash the boat down so it would look pretty.

"I will — don't worry. I ought to be home by ten at the latest. Go ahead and eat. Just save me something — okay?"

****

6:45 p.m.

Ann and Jerry Jensen showed up at the motel with enough sandwiches and cold drinks for everyone. Kim helped pass out the food and urged Amy Gressner to eat something.

"I can't right now, Kim. Don't worry about me, dear. I ate something earlier."

She nervously clenched her hands together as she talked and Kim clasped one of her hands in her own.

"Amy. Let's try to be positive, okay? Jason's a pretty tough little guy... "

At that, his mother started to cry again, and Kim was sorry she had said anything. Grant Gressner seemed unusually calm — like a warrior going into battle. Kim guessed that he had realistically appraised the situation, and that whatever was to happen tonight, he was trying to steel himself to deal with it emotionally.

Captain Gates arrived at the motel just then, looking a little more rested than he had. He had a new sheaf of papers in his hand.

"Info on Mitch Foler," he said as he walked into the room. "We got a lead on his sister in California. I want to know everything there is to know about this guy. Maybe somewhere in his background will be a clue that will help us to sort out this mess."

****

7:00 p.m.
Yuba City, California

Forty-nine year old Clarise Stead backed her 1981 Honda out of the garage. As was usual for July, it was a hot night.

She could almost bear any amount of heat in the day if it cooled at night. For a brief moment, she thought of her childhood in Warrenton, Oregon. There, she and her brother Mitch used to walk out toward the Army base, Fort Stevens in the evenings.

In the waning daylight, they'd play cowboys and Indians. Mitch's favorite place was on top of the old Army bunkers. He used to pretend they were forts and he was defending them.

But that was a long time ago — back in the fifties. She hadn't heard from Mitch in over ten years. In the meantime, her own husband, Stan, had passed away, and she had retired from her job as school custodian due to health problems. Her monthly disability check sustained her — sort of. She spent her days being lonely and trying to beat the heat.

The evening show at the Star Theater was starting in fifteen minutes. At least they would have air conditioning, and maybe by the time she got home around 9:30, there would be a breeze.

Chapter 21

The Drop

Wednesday, July 1st 7:30 p.m.
Astoria

Wednesday night was a replay of Tuesday except in slow motion. An unmarked auto carrying an F.B.I. agent, Captain Gates, and the bag of money made its way down the shore access road. Captain Gates, accompanied by two Coast Guardsmen, would take the money out in the small runabout to the waiting buoy. Marc would wait on shore after making sure the transceiver was on and in working order. It would be Captain Gates who would actually attach the bag to the floating metal structure.

Farther west in town, the Gressners once again waited by the designated phone booth. For now, they were sitting in the police car. No one expected a call for at least two hours. Amy Gressner got out of the car frequently to take short walks around the parking lot. She shaded her eyes with her hand and stared northward... as though she could see what was happening two miles away.

****

7:45 p.m.

Ann Jensen sat in her pickup truck with Patches. Two other search dogs had arrived from Portland midday. Working with their handlers, they had searched some park areas close to town. Nobody had come up with even a hint of a trail. Ann had Patches with her now mainly for company. She was the one person of the Amateur Radio volunteer group who did not have a partner. Since she didn't plan to be involved in signal tracking, she was standing ready to help in any way needed. At the moment, she was sitting in the driveway, just monitoring some of the traffic going over the emergency net.

****

8:00 p.m.

Jon Adams finished washing off the last of the decks. His wife didn't need to remind him to "make it look pretty." The "Sea Maid" was his pride and joy, and he never ever left her for the night with even one rope out of place. He smiled to himself as he thought of her debut on television. He looked down the line of other fishing and pleasure boats in the marina and thought the tv guy must have known what he was doing. He'd picked the best ship in the lot. A few more scrubs and then at 8:45, he'd pull out for his brief trip of cinematic glory.

****

8:01 p.m.

Standing in the swaying runabout, Captain Gates reached out and grabbed hold of the buoy. The outboard was just idling and the Coast Guardsmen were trying to keep the craft steady for him as he reached out and fastened the straps of the bulky bag through the metal rings on the buoy. Satisfied that the ransom was above the water line, Captain Gates gave the signal to accelerate.

****

8:05 p.m.

"It's there," Mitch whispered into his cell phone.

****

8:10 p.m.

Clad in his wetsuit, " Orlando the Great," emerged from the shrubbery east of town. Bent over awkwardly under the weight of his tanks and weight belt, he scrambled down the rocky embankment and eased into the water. There wasn't a person in sight. Within seconds, he was submerged and swimming steadily toward his goal.

****

8:20 p.m.

Getting no answer by phone, Lieutenant Halverson drove out to the home of Clarice Stead. The house was dark. He peeked in the garage window. No car.

A neighbor watering his lawn watched the police officer with interest. He put down his hose and came over to the edge of the drive.

"Something wrong?"

"Do you know when Mrs. Stead will be back?"

"Not really. She said something about going to a movie - - you know, since it's so hot and all."

"Do you know which one?"

The man shrugged his shoulders and shook his head.

"Anything I can help you with?"

"No, we just need to ask her a couple of questions. It doesn't involve her — just some information we need. Here, I'll give you my card — would you give it to her, please."

"Sure thing, Officer."

Lieutenant Halversen drove away knowing Clarice Stead would most likely have to give a full explanation to her nosy neighbor. He called back to the station to relay his information. It would probably be a couple of hours before he could question Mrs. Stead. Within minutes, the message came back. 'Find her and talk to her now.'

There were four theaters in town. One of them was playing a Sci Fi horror movie. He dismissed that as the least likely and instructed headquarters to put in a call to each of the other three. If Clarice Stead were there, they would find her.

****

8:30 p.m.

Kim sat quietly in the back of the squad car, her radio to her ear. She knew that by now Marc had arrived at Captain Gates' location. If there was a land pursuit, he would ride with him. They were counting on Kim to call them, the minute the Gressners heard from the kidnapper... if they did.

****

8:40 p.m.

It was a harder swim than Orlando had anticipated. He hadn't realized how out of shape he was and this last half hour of fighting the current had just about exhausted him. He figured the hour's worth of air in his tank might be nearly gone.

It was completely dark under water and the small flashlight he held did little to illuminate the way. But there was no question as to the right direction — just keep swimming against the flow.

At 8:42, he eased up near the surface and chanced a glance south toward his goal. The night was clear and the sharp moon crescent etched itself against the deepening black of the sky. The old abandoned cannery on shore was his landmark and there it was two hundred yards dead ahead. Off to the right, barely visible to him, was the buoy, swaying gently in the evening sea.

****

8:45 p.m.

Here it was — his moment in time. Jon Adams backed his fishing vessel out of its marina berth and proceeded out to sea. He kind of expected that the television guy might have come back with final instructions, but he guessed he thought he had understood what he was to do.

Who knows? he thought happily as he sailed up past the Coast Guard station. Maybe there'll be other parts in other movies. This might be the start of something big. Maneuvering in close to the buoy was going to be a little difficult for his twenty-eight foot boat, but Jon knew the Sea Maid like an expert equestrian knows his mount. He planned on making the circle at as high speed as possible — make a show of it. For a thousand bucks, a little pizzazz wouldn't hurt.

****

8:52 p.m.

Mitch Foler was really tempted to stay in his perch on the bluff and watch the heist, but his fear of being caught in the confusion that would ensue immediately afterwards motivated him to move back toward his van. Better to be quite a ways up the coastline and be in position for Leo's call. This time tomorrow, he thought — this time tomorrow, they would be on their way to South America.

****

8:59 p.m.

They were coming for him again. Jason whimpered and drew himself up in a ball as tightly as his restraints would allow him. A rat ran over his legs, sinking his sharp teeth into his soft flesh as it passed by. Frantically, Jason thrust his legs out and then bent them back under him. He grabbed the rock between his hands. There was only one thought in his head.

"GO AWAY GO AWAY GO AWAY" He pounded the message rhythmically against the metal pipe. Dit Dit Dit Dah Dah Dah Dit Dit Dit.

158

Chapter 22

Pickup

Wednesday, July 1st 9:00 p.m.
Astoria

He was almost under the buoy. Orlando didn't dare a peek at this close range — felt his luck had changed when he saw the floating marker above him. Letting out air, he sank until he was ten feet under it. He was exhausted, and his air was running low. It took all of his concentration not to panic and bob to the surface.

Motionless in the darkness, he waited. Was that it? He strained to hear. Yes. The engine noise was coming closer. He descended a few more feet to be sure to be well below the boat's hull.

****

9:04 p.m.

"Here we go," Captain Gates said as calmly as NASA Control. "Let him get it and then we'll follow."

Marc sat tensely in his pickup truck, the captain beside him. They had elected his vehicle because of the tracking capabilities of his antennas. Parked up on the road with a clear view of the buoy, they were inconspicuous — especially in the darkness. Up until this minute, the two men had been silent — just listening to the reassuring intermittent output tone of the transmitter inside the money bag.

Captain Gates trained his binoculars on the fast approaching fishing boat.

"He's going to have to slow down to get it."

"Doesn't look like he is," Marc said. As he spoke he knew that Kim and the other ham radio operators were waiting expectantly to hear what was happening.

"Looks like we spooked him," the captain said.

Marc raised his binoculars to watch the fishing boat sweep around the buoy with such speed that its wake sent the rusty red marker jigging in the swells. He turned to the captain to see what the next plan of action was. The boat had made the turn and was headed west back toward the Coast Guard station.

"Follow them," was Captain Gate's calm order over his two way radio to the Coast Guardsmen down below.

"Wait a minute!" Marc said excitedly.

"What?"

"Listen! The signal's gone."

Both men instantly trained their binoculars on the buoy... which was still swaying crazily in the waves — except that now the green canvas bag hanging from its cross structure was gone.

"Could it have fallen off?"

"No way. I secured that bag myself."

"It has to be underwater," Marc argued.

"Why?"

"Because radio signals don't carry under water."

****

9:05 p.m.

Clarice Stead was at the second movie house the police called. Reluctantly, this theater manager, as had the one at the first theater, made an announcement over the movie's soundtrack.

"Excuse the interruption but we have an emergency call for Clarice Stead."

Within minutes, she was in the lobby, bewildered.

"What's wrong?"

"Ms. Stead, do you have a brother by the name of Mitch Foler?"

****

9:06 p.m.

"What's happening," Amy Gressner implored of Kim.

Kim held her transceiver out between them with the volume turned up so the Gressners could hear. Agent Lamar stood outside the car talking on his radio to other law enforcement personnel.

"Sounds like they're going to stop that boat wherever it was heading," Kim said. "And somehow someone has taken the money underwater."

"I just don't understand," Amy said.

****

9:07 p.m.

For a few minutes after Orlando grabbed the money bag with his black neoprene-gloved hand, he stayed motionless under the buoy, too scared to start moving. The bag had come loose with one snap, just as he'd requested. He was sure only the very top of his wetsuit hood came above the surface for a split second. Hopefully, people watching were too distracted by the speeding boat to focus on the buoy and the activity in the swirling water around it.

He couldn't afford to stay here long. Sucking up the last of his air, he struggled eastward along the bottom, lugging not only the weight of his equipment but also the seventy-five pound bag of money. One hundred yards up the river, the tank was dry.

Like he'd rehearsed in his mind over and over, Orlando released both his weight belt and the straps that held his air tank. The money bag provided just about the same amount of weight compensation as the equipment had, and he floated up to the same position beneath the surface he'd maintained on his swim down. He aimed his body higher, until his snorkel broke the surface.

After an explosive snort of air to clear the water from the snorkel, Orlando drew in his first breath of outside air in over an hour. It was too dark to see anything now, but there were no engine sounds behind him. That was a good sign

****
9:15 p.m.
Jon Adams waved to the two men in dark suits walking toward him as he guided the Sea Maid into her marina berth.

They were dressed up. Perhaps they were the Hollywood executives come to pay him for his television role. He tried to look nonchalant as he tied the vessel up and leaped from her deck onto the wharf.

Drying his hands off on his pants, he smiled and walked confidently toward them.

"Was that okay?"

"Was what okay?" one of them countered.

"My run up around the buoy. You are from the television station aren't you?"

"Television station?"

"Yeah, the one that needed somebody to make a run around the buoy — promoting Astoria and the magic festival and all."

Jon sounded exasperated as he talked, but when the two men pulled out F.B.I. identification cards, his mood completely sombered.

"What's going on here? I think I need some explanation."

"I think you do too," one of the agents said.

****
9:20 p.m.
Clarice Stead didn't really mind missing the movie — it wasn't that good anyway. She'd mainly come for the air conditioning. But when the police officer in the lobby told her why he was questioning her, she fervently wished she were still back inside in her seat.

Mitch.. oh Mitch, her heart said. It had been over a year since she'd had any word from him. She had hoped that somehow his life had straightened out. No, she told the lieutenant, she didn't have any knowledge of her brother's whereabouts. He never answered her letters — just a brief note last summer saying that he would be getting out soon, and that he might call her someday. He never had.

She cried openly as the lieutenant told her of his involvement in the Astoria kidnapping.

"Astoria! Why that's right near where we grew up."

"Ms. Stead, would you come on down to the office? We have some questions we want to ask you."

****

9:30 p.m.

Jason panted, both from fear and exertion. The hungry rats kept scrambling over his bare legs and it took all his strength to keep his legs moving. Harder and harder, he pounded with the tiny rock in his hands. But the rats were getting used to the sound. Occasionally, he caught a glint of their eyes in the dark — big and glowing and hungry.

****

9:35 p.m.

"AA7RW from KA7ITR. Please move east two blocks and wait there. Another volunteer will be joining you."

"KA7ITR from AA7RW. Understood. Moving now."

Captain Gates had requested the move. After the news had come in that the fishing ship captain was an innocent victim in the kidnapper's scheme, there were only two possibilities left. One — that somehow the wake of the boat had knocked the bag off. Divers with powerful flashlights were searching the area, but they wouldn't be able to know for sure until daylight, or Two — that a diver himself had picked up the money.

"And I bet he's moving east up the river — that's the way the current's going with high tide," the captain told Marc as they continued to wait on the bluff, monitoring the simplex frequency.

The same instructions as before were in force. If spotted, the kidnapper was not to be interfered with. Whatever chance still existed that he might make a call was the Gressner's only hope. Captain Gates turned his attention to his police radio as a call came in from headquarters.

****

9:37 p.m.

Just as the captain was discounting that hope, Jason's parents were clinging to it as their only thread.

"It's been forty-five minutes since he picked up the money," Amy Gressner said. For the moment she was clear-eyed, almost spacey, Kim thought. It was as though she had talked herself into believing that Orlando really would call, tell them where Jason was, and then everything would go back to being normal for their family.

"Yes, dear, he should call any minute now," her husband told her, but his eyes met with agent Lamar's as he spoke.

"KA7SJP from KA7ITR."

"Go ahead, Marc."

"Captain Gates is talking to one of your F.B.I. agents right now." Kim looked over and saw Lamar in the parking lot, his radio at his mouth. "Be prepared to go with him, Kim."

****

9:39 p.m.

After the hours of inactivity, it was almost a relief to be doing something. Agent Phil Lamar told the Gressners what had just happened. The Captain had received information that one of the kidnappers, Mitch Foler, had grown up in Warrenton, right near Fort Stevens. It seemed very possible that he might have hidden the boy there.

Lamar would wait at the phone booth with Mrs. Gressner. Ann Jensen was on her way now with her search dog to pick up Mr. Gressner and Kim. Other units would meet them at the fort to begin a search. If the kidnappers showed up there, they would be waiting for them — if they phoned, Amy Gressner would take the call — if they didn't do either... well, they would keep on searching.

****

9:50 p.m.

Orlando was shivering with fatigue. The heavy bag that he'd looped to a canvas belt around his waist bumped into his hips as he swam. He'd had to steady it with one hand, slowing him even more. He wondered if he was even halfway there. Swimming barely under the surface, he decided to risk a glance.

Dropping his feet so he was vertical in the water, Orlando grabbed his snorkel to flatten it against him. His face broke the water and he peered toward the coastline. A few lights from houses twinkled in the distance... and there... just ahead was the yellow marker light he'd spotted. Orlando slipped back under the water.

****

10:00 p.m.

He was less than a quarter mile from the main road. In the darkness of the trees that shielded his van, Mitch waited. In his right hand was the cellular phone that he hoped would ring soon.

Chapter 23

"Daddy... I'm scared!"

Wednesday, July 1st 10:05 p.m.
Astoria

"He's back topside," Marc whispered in the quiet of the truck cab as the transmit signal reappeared.

Captain Gates' eyes met Marc's as a steady tone for five seconds and then thirty seconds of silence began its repetitive cycle.

"Okay, let's get a fix on it," the captain said. "But tell everyone to go easy."

"The fox is back," Marc transmitted to the waiting group of Amateur Radio operators.

What they had often practiced as a game of fox and hounds (the hounds being hams with antennas who enjoyed tracking and fixing the location of a hidden transmitter) was now being played out in earnest. And everyone in this volunteer group knew what the prize for this hunt was — the possibility of saving a boy's life.

****

10:08 p.m

Orlando shed his wetsuit in record time, not feeling the skin and hair it pulled as he ripped off the black neoprene. No time to bother hiding the diving gear; he yanked on the jeans, sweatshirt, and tennis shoes in less than a minute. Shouldering the heavy money bag, he called Mitch on the cell phone as he made his way up to the road.

A bulky shore pine hid him until he saw the van's headlights. Thirty seconds later, Orlando was in the front seat and he and Mitch were speeding west along Highway 30 toward the bridge to Washington.

10:10 p.m.

It was everyone's guess that if the kidnapper made his escape by car, that he would go east on Highway 30 toward Portland. The information about Mitch and Fort Stevens had done little to change that opinion. The kid might indeed be there, but no one seriously believed that Orlando would be going back through the congested Astoria area for him.

Thus, Amateur Radio operators and law enforcement officials positioned themselves in a couple of locations east of the drop site. At the resumption of the signal, Marc and Captain Gates pulled onto the highway.

"Either we're going the wrong way or he's not moving," Marc said. They had barely moved half a mile eastward. "The signal's getting stronger."

Captain Gates had Marc pull over to the side of the road while Marc listened to reports from other monitoring stations. Everyone confirmed his opinion. The vehicle, whatever it was, was going back toward town.

"You suppose he is going back for the kid?"

"I highly doubt it, but let's give him his space," the captain replied.

Marc watched the needle on his signal strength meter peak as a dark van passed them on the highway. Marc and Captain Gates waited anxiously for the next five second transmission.

"Not as loud — agree?"

"I agree," Captain Gates said.

Marc started his truck. They were five cars behind the van.

10:15

Marc was busy running the net directing ham radio operators, but the first transmission he made was to Kim.

She told the Gressners what had just happened. Amy Gressner still seemed to be in her dream-like state.

"Well then he's coming back here to turn Jason loose. Soon this will all be over."

She got out of the car and stood next to the telephone — surely, it would ring soon. The F.B.I. agent watched her with pity.

****

10:16

Captain Gates needed a few more hands and ears. He was , listening to the incoming transmissions Marc was monitoring, listening to the transmit tone from the money bag, and trying to talk to headquarters all at the same time.

He was also giving directions to various unmarked police cars situated throughout the area. To everyone — volunteers and official personnel alike — the directive was the same. Try to keep the suspect van in view but do nothing to stop them.

****

10:20

"Where do you want to start?" Ann Jensen questioned the deputies who had already arrived at the gate to Fort Stevens.

"The bunkers," one of them said. He held a map in his hand. "We've checked with the security people here, and they suggested we try the communications one out near the gate. It's the only area that's not part of the tours."

****

10:21 p.m.

They were going to eat him! Jason half-screamed, his parched mouth fighting against the gag, as one of the creatures sank its teeth into his leg. Frantically, he pounded

his hand holding the rock against the pipe. GO AWAY GO
... the rock fell from his hand.

****

10:23 p.m.

"Oh no," Captain Gates said. "They're turning toward the bridge."

"You want to talk to them?"

Marc held the borrowed transceiver in his hand. Captain Gates' brow furrowed with concentration.

"Not yet. I'll alert Washington State Police. We don't want to stop them yet — not as long as there's any chance for the kid."

****

10:24 p.m.

While Mitch focused on driving and watching the rearview mirror, Orlando explored the money bag.

"Looks like it's all in hundreds. Guess that'll spend as well as anything in South America."

"Don't be spending it yet, Leo. We've gotta get out of this place first."

"They're not gonna touch us, Mitch. They think we're going for the kid. Then once we get across that bridge, we'll just sort of disappear on the backroads and make our way back to Portland."

"Yeah, Leo — that's the plan, that's the plan."

He gripped the steering wheel hard as he made the turn onto 101 leading toward the bridge spanning the Columbia River.

****

10:25 p.m.

"Seek Patches, Seek!"

The black and white dog buried her nose in the sweater belonging to Jason and began casting around at the road's edge.

"The scent's pretty old by now, isn't it?" Kim questioned Ann.

"Yeah it is, but it's better than nothing. She'll search for just a human scent anyway whether she has a clue to go on."

Several sheriff's deputies had joined them and were walking through the heavily treed area, shining their flashlights along the ground. Patches ran erratically along the edge of the concrete bunker which extended above ground through much of the area. Suddenly with an excited whine, the dog scrambled to the top of the structure.

"She smells something," Ann said. "Come on!"

The others needed no urging — they clambered up some cement steps which led to the flat top surface. Patches stopped by a protruding metal vent pipe. She whined and began pawing at it.

"Jason?" Kim called down the opening.

****

10:26 p.m.

There was a trick Jason's brain had learned in the last two days. When he couldn't keep the creatures away by himself, he could keep himself away from the creatures. Something had just bitten him and he could hear noise up above him — bigger creatures! It was time to get away. He closed his eyes tight and willed himself to sleep — away from the scary things — away from everything. He wanted so much to sleep, but something was calling to him — the creatures? Clawing through the dirt, his fingers struck and then grasped the rock. GO AWAY, GO AWAY, GO AWAY — he put all his strength into beating out the staccato message.

****

10:27 p.m.

"What the?" Mitch grumbled as a car four vehicles ahead of him stalled just at the bridge access.

"Don't honk," Orlando warned as Mitch pushed the palm of his hand against the steering column. "Looks like they're getting it started."

Mitch put his head out the window to peer ahead. A man had the hood open of the stopped car, a weatherbeaten station wagon. While the woman driver cranked the ignition, he signaled her with his hand. Mitch and Orlando heard the engine catch. The man slapped down the hood and climbed back in.

****

10:28 p.m.

"You know, I really don't want them to get across into Washington," Captain Gates said.

"Just say the word," Marc said, holding his transceiver.

"What word?" Captain Gates asked bitterly. "What are we going to say — you're surrounded?"

"KA7ITR from KA7SJP — Marc!"

"What, Kim?"

Her excited voice coming over the frequency Marc was monitoring on his dash-mounted rig filled the truck cab.

"We've found him!!"

"Alive?"

"Yes! Listen!"

The soft husky voice of Jason was clearly audible. He was whimpering but he was talking too.

"Kim! Switch your rig to the simplex frequency and put the mike in front of Jason's mouth. Do it now!"

Captain Gates' mouth opened in surprise. There was a little bit of rustling and then Jason.

****

10:30 p.m.

"Almost there," Orlando said, watching the line of traffic ahead. They were back up to speed — going about fifty and two thirds of the way across the bridge.

"Daddy, I'm scared..."

The tearful voice of Jason flowed out of the money bag.

Orlando was too horror-stricken to speak. He turned and clutched Mitch's arm with a death grip.

"You idiot!" Mitch screamed at him, but it was too late. The van swerved, crashing through the metal barriers.

****

"My God!" Captain Gates whispered.

He slammed on his brakes as did the line of traffic ahead of him. For the next horrifying thirty seconds, they watched as the kidnappers' van plummeted through open air and down to the waiting Columbia River.

Chapter 24

Celebrations

Saturday, July 4th
Astoria

"Are they going to shoot off really big fireworks, Kim?"

"You bet, Jason. And we're going to see them all. That nice officer from the Coast Guard made sure we had front row seats. And guess what? The man who actually lights the fuses is a ham radio operator too — WA6ILQ. He said he'd make this show especially good just for you."

The small boy, still with a few bandages on his legs, crawled comfortably up in Kim's lap and leaned back, ready to see the show. He had just gotten out of the community hospital this afternoon — was still a little weak from his ordeal.

Except for wanting a light on while he slept, he seemed to be suffering few ill effects from the kidnapping trauma. The doctors who treated him told his parents that kids were remarkably resilient — however, they needed to be alert to emotional problems that might surface later on.

Kim turned to look down the dock. Marc was just coming back from the pavilion. The Fourth of July music performance had been wonderful — patriotic, lively, and fun. Tomorrow, he would go back to Portland, Kim would return to Salem, and the Gressners would fly home to be reunited with their daughters.

"Hey, Jason — how's it going?"

"Hi. Can I sit in your lap for awhile, Daddy?"

Kim smiled up at Amy and Grant Gressner who had just arrived after meeting with Captain Gates. Jason crawled across the chairs as his father sat down and snuggled into his arms.

"Deserted by a handsome young man," Kim said, laughing.

Jason looked over at her and stuck out one hand so he could hang onto hers while still clinging to his father with the other. She put his tiny fist to her lips and kissed it and then stood up as Marc approached.

"Jason, I'll be right back, okay? There's another handsome young man I want to talk to for a few minutes."

"That would be me, of course," said Marc giving a mock bow.

"You two run along. We can never thank you enough," Amy Gressner said.

Kim took Marc's hand and they walked down the boardwalk.

"You know it's amazing that Jason's mom has gotten over this so well."

"Yeah, I know — the night of the kidnapping she was just so spacey — well it was really scary, but now she seems pretty much okay," agreed Kim.

"How's his dad?"

"Okay — he hasn't said much to me, but I heard him tell Captain Gates that being able to confront Orlando as he was pulled out of the water was the best therapy in the world."

"I wonder why he survived and Mitch didn't?" Marc mused.

"I don't know, but he's going to have a long time to think about it in prison."

They stopped to watch a flotilla of small boats sailing toward the harbor, colorful American flags flying from their masts. By now, everyone along the coast had heard of the dramatic ending to the kidnapping — the safe retrieval of the money bag by Coast Guard divers — the rescue of Jason. This was going to be the biggest Fourth of July Astoria had ever seen. The Gressners were given the official key to the city and tonight the fireworks celebration put on jointly by the Coast Guard and the Fire Department were being done in Jason's honor.

"What have you got?"

"A couple of envelopes the Gressners just gave me," Kim said. "One of them's to you."

"And one's to you."

"You go first."

"No, you." Kim insisted.

Laughing, Marc tore the end of the long white envelope open and pulled out a letter and a check.

"Oooh," he whistled. "It's for a thousand bucks."

"Read the letter."

"Okay. 'Dear Marc Lawrence. On behalf of the First Bank of Los Angeles, please accept this reward in compensation for your radio which was damaged in the Columbia River. We are grateful for your ingenuity in finding a way to save our money (and it was fine after it dried out!) but most of all for saving the life of Jason Gressner.'"

Marc looked down at Kim.

"Is that enough or do you want to hear more compliments about me. Hey, what's in yours?"

She tore the envelope open. It was a letter from the Gressners and it contained a check also for a thousand dollars. With tears in her eyes, Kim read the letter aloud.

"Dear Kim: Before you say you won't take this, let us say that we want you to buy yourself a tiny radio just like Marc's. We can't thank the two of you enough and we'd like to be part of furnishing the technology that will let you talk to each other even more. As soon as we recover from all of this, we all plan to get our ham radio licenses. Jason says knowing SOS saved him from the creatures. I think the fact that you taught him code gave him a way to save his own precious mind. You're a dear and we all love you.

The Gressners — Grant, Amy, Julianna, Stacie, and Jason."

"Oh Kim — don't cry. Hey look, the fireworks are starting."

Down at the wharf, a cannon boomed and the sky lit up with glowing red, white, and blue stars.

"Think you might have some time this week to spend with me?" Marc asked as he bent to kiss her gently.

"You can count on it," Kim said.

Author's Note

On a cruise several years ago with my stepmother, the late W6NAZ, I got the idea of a story about a kidnapping aboard a ship. Where would the victim be held? How would the ransom be delivered? I visited the radio room a couple of times and managed to get "lost" in the crew quarters. In the brief time before I was escorted out, I didn't really see any place where "Jason" could be hidden. So I decided that the kidnapping should take place in port in Astoria on the beautiful Oregon coast.

Before you write me to say that big cruise ships don't dock in Astoria, let me assure you that I know that. However, I believe due to the wonderful sightseeing available in the Astoria-Seaside area, that someday they will.

I hope you enjoy this story, my fifth effort at combining fiction and ham radio.

Heartfelt thanks to the following individuals for their help.

Steve Jensen, W6RHM
Dick and Mary Lutz
Hollie Molesworth, KA7SJP
Dick Ritterband, AA6BC
Brigitte Rolph
My family — Dave, Michael, and Bob Wall
Heidi Wheland
Robert Williams, M.D.

73,

Cynthia Wall KA7ITT

Cynthia Wall